THE DETECTIVE'S DATE

CONTEMPORARY CHRISTIAN ROMANCE

FULLER FAMILY IN BRUSH CREEK ROMANCE

BOOK FOUR

LIZ ISAACSON

ISBN-13: 978-1638760900

"Happy is the man that findeth wisdom, and the man that getteth understanding."

Proverbs 3:13

CHAPTER 1

"Come on, BB, hurry it up." Kyler Fuller held the door to the cabin open with his foot, his hands stuffed full of grocery sacks. His muscles strained against the plastic bags as the horizon boiled with dark gray clouds, as thunder boomed and crashed and threatened to make the sky fall.

The eight-year-old Welsh corgi somehow got his stumpy legs up to the front porch and through the door before the rain started falling. Kyler ducked in after him, glad he'd made it to the cabin before the weather.

He'd come up last night and stacked wood in the mudroom after McDermott—his best friend and now one of his sister's husbands—had alerted him to the forecast.

Kyler busied himself with putting the groceries away, missing the way his long hair used to sway with the simplest of tasks. But he had been able to get more dates since cleaning up his appearance. Now he shaved every day, and kept his hair clipped as if he were about to enlist in the armed forces.

He worked out enough mowing lawns and moving pavers that he didn't worry about adding running to his regimen. He'd tried getting out to the summer picnics this year, the speed dating event at the church, and hanging out with his friends and brothers at the karaoke bar on the weekends.

Sure, he'd gotten some attention. But not from anyone he cared to continue a relationship with.

"BB," he scolded as the dog started licking the cabinet. "Knock it off." He chuckled as the corgi seemed to give him a smile and then went right back to the cabinet, where something must've been spilled in the past.

His phone rang, but he ignored the call from his oldest brother, instead tapping out an *I made it before the rain* in response to Milton. Since another of his brothers, Brennan, had moved to California, Milt had become Kyler's wingman.

But Kyler had had enough for a while. He'd come to the family cabin up in the hills above Brush Creek, where he planned to stay for the next few days. The fishing, hiking, and relaxing would've been better if the weather was more cooperative, but June in this part of Utah was unpredictable at best.

And "Hail," Kyler said with wonder, at worst.

The sound of the hard hail on the roof and windows upset BB, who whimpered. Kyler scooped him up and held the brown and white dog to his chest. "All right, Bread and Butter. You're fine." He chuckled as the dog shook in his arms. He set the little dog on the counter and pulled out a pound of ground beef.

That got BB to hold still, and as the symphony of hail continued to beat down on the house, he seasoned the meat with salt, pepper, and garlic powder. With the grill pan heating on the stove, harder pounding sounded from the front door.

Kyler jerked his head toward the door, his heart leaping to the back of his throat. There was someone out in this storm? This far from civilization?

"Hello?" Desperation rode in the word. More banging came on the door, and then someone tried to open it. Kyler didn't remember locking the door, but the knob didn't turn. That was when he realized he was just standing there in the kitchen, while someone was trapped outside in the relentless hail.

"Just a second!" He dashed toward the door, hoping his little dog didn't waddle off the countertop of go after the raw ground beef.

He fumbled with the lock and yanked open the door to find a waterlogged person standing there. Kyler blinked, surprised to see the curve of a woman's body inside the police uniform.

All beige, the pants ended in black boots. She wore a belt cinched around her trim waist, and when her dark eyes met Kyler's, he sucked in a breath. "Dahlia?"

"Can I come in?" she asked, her voice raspy as her chest heaved.

"Have you been running?"

"It's coming down out here," she said, still panting.

"Come in, come in." Kyler stepped back to let Dahlia Reid enter the cabin. She took off her flat-brimmed hat and let the water drip to the floor. Kyler didn't mind, but he had no idea what to do with her. He mowed lawns, trimmed bushes, and built retaining walls for a living. He didn't know what to do with beautiful, soaked detectives.

"I'm—uh—making dinner. You want something to eat?" That sounded like a good idea. Food. Water. Shelter. The bare necessities of life. He stepped past her and managed to save the bowl of seasoned beef just before BB got his snout into it.

"We have a washer and dryer here too. We could get your clothes dry."

Dahlia wandered a little closer, her boots squeaking against the hard floor as she continued to drip water everywhere. "How big is this place?"

"Pretty big," he said. "We used to come up here for family vacations in the winter."

"All nine of you?"

"Eleven," he said. "My parents came too." He flashed her a smile, glad he didn't have to explain to her about his huge family. She used to be one of the patrol officers in the Brush Creek Police Department, and she was well-acquainted with Dawn especially. His wildest sister, Dawn had gotten in the most trouble growing up.

But Kyler didn't know Dahlia Reid. He just knew *of* her, the same way she knew of him and his family.

"Do you think there might be something I can change into while my clothes go through the wash?" Dahlia ran her fingers through her hair, combing some water from the curly ends.

Kyler stared at her, sure she was a dark-haired angel straight from heaven. His mind seemed stuck on someone he'd known about but had never seen.

"Kyler?" she asked, cocking her head to the side and training those dark as pitch eyes on him.

He shook himself out of this stupor and said, "Oh, yeah, probably." The scent of a too-hot pan met his nose and he hurried to turn down the heat under the grill pan. "Let's see, um, my sisters used to sleep in the first couple of rooms just down that hall. Feel free to look around and see what you can find."

Dahlia flashed him a brilliant smile that didn't quite reach her eyes, and turned toward the hall that led to the back of the cabin. She disappeared through the doorway, and Kyler stared at the ground beef and picked up a handful of it to make burgers.

"Idiot," he whispered. "You should've gone with her to find some clothes." But he couldn't go charging after her now. He adjusted the flame under the grill pan and got the meat sizzling.

BB yipped, but Kyler ignored him. The dog's claws

clicked on the countertop and he paced, paced, paced back and forth, giving a gargled yip every time he turned.

"I know," Kyler said, keeping an eye on the arched doorway that led to the hall. "I should've gone to help her." With all the burgers on the grill, he washed up real quick and rounded the peninsula in the island in favor of approaching the hall.

"Detective?" he called, slowing his steps as he neared the first doorway that led to a bedroom where his sisters used to sleep. The noise from the hail quieted the farther he moved into the cabin, and he listened for Dahlia's reply.

"Dahlia?" He liked the way her name rolled off his tongue.

"Coming," she called. A few seconds later, the next door down opened and she came out, her fingers still working through her hair. A smile ghosted across her mouth. "I found a few things that will do."

She wore a pair of loose pajama pants the color of mint toothpaste, and a T-shirt that had a bright red U on it for the University of Utah. Both items were too big and hung off her lithe frame. She might be thin, but she was wiry, strong, and tough. At least if his brother-in-law Tate was to be believed.

Dahlia had trained Tate when he'd first come to town, right before she was made detective for the Unified Police Unit that covered several of the small towns out here west of Vernal.

And that was the bulk of what Kyler knew about her.

What he wanted to know seemed bottomless, and he quirked a smile at her. "Where are your wet clothes? I'll get them going. And I've got dinner started."

"Will there be cheese on the burgers?" She stepped back into the bedroom and returned a moment later with an armful of her wet clothes.

"Of course," he said.

"Good." She smiled at him and pushed the clothes into his hands as she passed. "I love cheese."

He chuckled and followed her back into the front part of the house, where the large living room attached to the dining room and the kitchen where he'd been working spread before him.

"Make yourself at home." He went through the door closest to the bar and opened the washing machine. The cupboard above the appliance held the detergent pods, and he got her laundry started.

He paused in the doorway to find her sitting on the couch, her back to him, her fingers plaiting her hair as she hummed. The song tickled something in his memory, but he couldn't quite place it.

The scent of cooking beef met his nose and he lunged around the peninsula and flipped the burgers, the pan hissing and spitting when the juices and raw meat met the hot surface. If he let them go longer than another sixty seconds, they'd be overdone.

He unwrapped the cheese quickly and splashed a bit of water on the grill pan and placed a big lid over the burgers to get the cheese nice and melty. He hadn't had time to get any of the toppings ready, but he flipped the flame off under the grill pan and removed the burgers to a plate to rest.

He'd never had a problem talking to women, and he sliced tomatoes as he asked, "So, Dahlia, where are you from?" He wasn't sure of her exact age, but she had to be close to his thirty-five. And she hadn't grown up here in Brush Creek.

"Vernal." She looked over her shoulder. "My parents still live there." Dahlia got up and sauntered over to the counter and leaned against it. "Can I help?"

"Oh, I'm fine," he said, reaching for the head of lettuce. "Do you have siblings?"

"Nope. Just me." Her smile seemed tight around the edges, and Kyler turned away from her to get out the ketchup, mustard, and mayo from the fridge.

"Toasted bun or no?"

"It's fine as-is."

"Then we're ready to eat." Kyler wasn't sure how long the storm would last, but when he glanced out the window, it was definitely still coming down strong. "At least the hail's stopped."

"Yeah." Dahlia started doctoring up her bun and Kyler copied her.

"So why were you out here?" he asked, knifing some mayo from the jar.

"Police business," she said, her tone guarded.

"Police business?" Surprise bolted through him. "Out this far?"

Dahlia lifted her eyes to meet his, no fear or hint of frustration in them at all. Her expression was quite unreadable and it sparked something deep inside Kyler's chest.

"Yes, out this far." Her words carried a double meaning, and Kyler got the hint.

None of your business.

Dahlia turned away and took her burger to the long picnic-style table in the dining room. Kyler wanted to ask more questions, but he wasn't sure he wanted to see Dahlia get upset. So he zipped his lips—except to open his mouth and take a big bite of his burger.

CHAPTER 2

Dahlia regretted the way she'd spoken to Kyler. She didn't have anything against the man. She simply didn't want to talk about her case. *Couldn't* talk about it.

"Thank you for dinner," she said, hoping to take the sting out of his expression.

He nodded, his mouth full of food. He had a good air about him, and Dahlia couldn't stop her gaze from wandering toward him and catching. He almost felt magnetic he exuded so much charisma. She liked his shorter haircut, though she certainly hadn't minded the long-haired version of him either. Dahlia had always had a thing for men with long hair.

Which is why you're not married.

Her mother's voice sprang into her head, unbidden, but loud nonetheless. Her very traditional, almost seventy-year-old mother did not approve of long hair on men, and when Dahlia had brought home Eric Hawkins to meet her folks, all she heard about for weeks was that his hair was too long.

Every man she brought home had some flaw, and at thirty-seven, Dahlia was beginning to wonder if she should just find someone she liked instead of trying to make sure her parents would approve of her husband.

Problem was, all she had were her parents. Without any siblings to bounce ideas off of, her parents were her whole world. And if they didn't like her husband, she felt like she'd be losing part of herself.

"Where'd you learn to cook?" she asked.

"My grandmother," he said. "She brought us kids over to her place one at a time. She taught Jazzy to dance, and Milt to sing, and me to cook." Kyler smiled with the memories only he could see in his mind's eye, but Dahlia appreciated the warmth in his voice.

She ate, glad when the silence between them wasn't too awkward. His little dog whined from the counter, and he got up to retrieve him.

"What's his name?" she asked.

"Bread and Butter," Kyler said. "BB for short."

The pup sort of looked like bread and butter, with toasty brown fur in some places, and white in others. "I have a cat named Ally."

"Clever," he said, reaching for his glass of punch.

She finished her burger and said, "I need to call in. Will you excuse me for a minute?"

"Of course."

She put her plate in the sink, very aware of the way the too big clothes hung off her slight shoulders and narrow waist. She could also feel the weight of Kyler's stare on her as she walked toward the bedroom where she'd left her radio. It had been crackly and full of static before the storm, but now that Mother Nature had settled on rain instead of hail, Dahlia hoped she could let her partner know she'd made it to safety. She hoped Gray had made it somewhere before the storm hit too.

With the door closed and locked—not that she thought Kyler would come barging in unannounced—Darla picked up her radio and moved to the window. Rain and wind danced a dangerous tango, splashing and lashing against the glass every few seconds.

"Gray," she said. "Come back, Gray. It's Dahlia." She released the button and waited. She swore half her life—on and off the job—was spent waiting. She'd almost become accustomed to it, like everything required the level of paperwork the police department did.

When he hadn't responded in a full minute, she tried again. "Gray. Come back, Gray. It's Dahlia. I made it to a cabin about a mile northwest from where we split. Where are you?"

They'd both known it was going to rain that day. The clouds had been predicting it for hours. But she'd found a trail they needed to follow before the weather washed it away. To speed things up, they'd gone in different directions, searching—always searching—for what they needed.

Right now, Dahlia needed to know her partner was okay. She tried one more time, sure that if his radio was working, he'd have answered by now. When he didn't, worry settled in her very bones and she stared out the window, trying to find a solution that kept her warm and dry.

Maybe he'd made it back to the car. Maybe he'd been trying to get in touch with her while she flirted with a Brush Creek local. Dahlia shook her head, her curls brushing against her neck as she did.

No, she hadn't been flirting. Dahlia didn't even quite know how to flirt. Sure, she'd dated over the years, but nothing had ever gotten too serious with anyone. She was too friendly, she'd been told. Or not friendly enough. Too masculine. Too feminine. She'd been told it all. And anytime things did get semi-serious and she brought them home to meet her parents, her mother had something snide to say that made Dahlia see the man in a different light.

Which was her own fault, she supposed. She didn't have to take what her mom said quite so deep into her heart.

She turned away from the window and took her radio with her as she walked back into the living room. Kyler had finished eating too, and now he sat at the table, his broad shoulders hunched over as he studied something in front of him.

He really was a magnificent specimen of a man, and she wondered how no one had snatched him up a decade ago. Dahlia didn't quite know his exact age, but single, eligible men in their thirties were hard to find in a small town.

And yet, there one sat. And he was employed, kind, and knew how to cook. She watched him for a while longer, wondering what strange rhythm her heart had decided to beat. She also hoped he had enough food for her to stay awhile, because "It doesn't look like it's going to let up any time soon," she said to announce her arrival back in the living room.

Kyler's shoulders straightened and he looked over one of them. "Milt said it might go into tomorrow. Snow, even, especially up here." He didn't sound happy about that.

"And you came up anyway?" she asked. "What were your weekend plans?"

He turned his whole body sideways on the chair so he could keep facing her. A frown pulled at his eyebrows and disappointment cut through his dark blue eyes. They reminded her of the dark wash blue jeans, comfortable and functional, but a piece of clothing that could also make a man.

Surprised at her accelerating pulse, Dahlia opted for a seat on the couch so she wouldn't be tempted to touch Kyler.

"Hiking, fishing, camping," he said.

"I saw your motorcycle out front," she said. "That's why I came knocking during the storm. You brought up equipment for all of that on a bike?"

"We have most of the that kind of stuff here already." He rose, his tall frame exuding confidence and charm, and came to sit closer to her. Not on the couch, but in an armchair at a ninety-degree angle from where she sat.

She saw a book open on the table, a pencil discarded beside it. "Studying?"

A laugh rumbled from his chest, and Dahlia couldn't help the way her attention riveted on him. She told herself to look away, keep a straight face.

But her emotions eradicated the rational thoughts in her mind. She giggled too, absorbing the happiness in his crooked smile and the way his eyes crinkled around the edges.

"Relaxing," he said. "Well, as best as I can without getting outside." He nodded toward the open book on the table. "That's a crossword puzzle book. My mother used to make us do all kinds of things when we came to the cabin. No TV. No radio." The smile slipped from his face, and Dahlia mourned the loss of it.

"Sometimes the silence is nice," he admitted. "Sometimes it drives me crazy."

"I understand that." More than Dahlia wanted to admit. Her house sat at the end of a cul-de-sac in a neighborhood with mostly people over the age of sixty. Sometimes the quiet atmosphere was welcome, especially after a long day at her desk, with ringing phones and people talking and constant activity.

But sometimes...sometimes silence smothered her,

pressed the life from her lungs, demanded she pay attention to it.

He exhaled like he was trying to clear his mind of something. "So there's plenty to do here. Games, puzzles, even needlepoint. Do you knit, Dahlia?"

She laughed this time, startling slightly when she saw the flirtatious twinkle in Kyler's blue jean eyes. No way he could be flirting with her. Could he?

"I am as far from a knitter as a person can get," she said.

"My mom taught me," he said, looking at his hands. "But I don't think my hands were quite made for it."

"They do seem better equipped for bigger things," she agreed, cursing herself for the statement. What did that even mean? She tore her gaze from his strong, capable hands, her face heating.

"Well, I think we'll be here for the night." He stood. "I'm going to go check the bedrooms. Make sure we have all the blankets we need."

Dahlia stood too. "Really? All night?"

Kyler lifted one eyebrow. "Listen." He cocked his head, his eyes drifting closed. He was beautiful in that moment. Soft. The sound of his slow inhalation in calmed her, and she let herself listen too.

"I don't know what I'm supposed to be hearing," she finally said, her voice half as loud as it usually was.

"Exactly." His eyes came open. "No hail on the roof. No rain on the window." He pointed to the glass on the far side of the room. "It's snowing."

Chapter 3

Kyler didn't know if he should be grateful for the snow, or frustrated by it. If he'd been in the cabin alone, he'd have been irritated and moody. But with Dahlia there....

He opened the linen closet and pulled out an armful of towels, the scent of her hair still teasing his nose. *Help me take care of her*, he prayed. Though the detective could surely take care of herself, Kyler was happy she'd stumbled upon the cabin during the storm.

"Are you sure you have enough food for me?" She joined him and took the towels from him. Standing so close to her in the hall made every cell in Kyler's body vibrate.

"'Course there is." His voice grated against itself and he cleared the emotion from it. "I brought a lot. Hiking and fishing tend to work up an appetite."

She smiled up at him, the action reaching all the way

to her eyes this time. They lit up from within, and Kyler felt like he was looking into the windows of a beautiful soul.

"Are you dating anyone?" The words left his mouth before he'd had time to think them through. Horror struck him right behind his breastbone, especially when her eyes widened and she sucked in a sharp breath.

Kyler grabbed the first blanket he could get his hands on and retreated down the hall. "Sorry," he mumbled, hoping the apology would reach her. "None of my business." He paused at the doorway to the room where he'd been planning to sleep. "You'll be in the green room?"

She pointed to the room from which she'd emerged earlier. "Is this the green room?"

"Yeah." His chuckle sounded so nervous, and he hated it and liked it at the same time. Maybe he didn't need to dance around Dahlia. "Bathroom right there across the hall." He indicated the door next to the closet where they'd been standing. "You can put the towels in there."

"And you'll be in there."

"Well, not right this second. I'm going to make sure things are ready and then build a big fire. It'll keep the whole cabin toasty all night."

Alarm crossed her face. "There's no heat here?"

"No central air or heat, no," he said, a shiver running down his arms from the draft in the bunk bed room. "Your room is close to the fireplace. Or you can sleep on the couch if you want."

Dahlia looked over her shoulder. "We'll see."

Kyler nodded, the pressure building in his chest to blurt out something crazy again. He ducked his head and had taken one step into the bedroom when she said, "I'm not seeing anyone right now, no."

A smile struck his face like lightning, and his step faltered, but he continued into the bedroom. With nothing to do—his mother kept the beds clean and made—but put the extra blanket on the bottom bunk he'd be sleeping in, he went back into the hall to catch Dahlia walking into the bathroom.

He hurried past and back to the kitchen and living room. Before he brought in the wood to build a fire, he switched her clothes from the washer to the dryer so she'd have them in the morning. Then he set about using his Boy Scout skills to get a roaring fire going in the hearth.

He loved the cheery sight of dancing flames, enjoyed the smoky, ashy smell of the fire, and sat back on his haunches to watch the powerful force flicker.

"Do you have coffee?" Dahlia asked, drawing Kyler's attention and making him realize how warm his face had become.

He leapt to his feet when she continued behind the couch and into the kitchen as if she'd make it. "Yeah, we do. I can do it."

"You made dinner." She flashed him a smile as he crowded into the small space with her. "I can make coffee." She glanced around for the machine.

"It's right here." He dragged the fancy coffee maker his brother's wife had given his parents for Christmas a year or two ago. "It's one of those that you put the little cups in?" Why he phrased that as a question, he wasn't sure.

"Oh." Dahlia's brows creased, and she looked up at him. Something delicious and slow moved through him, heating him the same way the joyful flames had. She swallowed, a nervous glint to her eye. "Did you hear what I said in the hallway?"

"Yeah." His voice sounded like he'd rubbed it against sandpaper. He cleared it so he wouldn't give too much away—as if he hadn't already. "I mean, yes. Yes, I heard you."

A smile lit her whole countenance. "So maybe you'd like to take me to dinner?"

"Maybe." He reached into a cupboard and pulled down a tray filled with coffee cups, hot chocolate cups, and even apple cider cups. "Pick your poison."

She studied the little cups, her now-dry hair brushing her forearm as she lifted it to choose one. "I love hot chocolate."

Kyler took the cup from her and popped it into the machine, filled it with water, and faced her again. "How about I get your phone number? Then we can make plans for when we can go out."

"Do you have cell service out here?" she asked.

"Yeah, sure."

She sucked in a breath. "A phone?"

He gestured toward the counter where he'd cut tomatoes and avocadoes. "Right there."

"I need to call in."

She hadn't said she'd give her phone number to him after that, but he nodded. "Sure, of course. I'll babysit this for you." Not that it needed babysitting. The machine did all the work.

Dahlia snatched the phone from the counter and dialed as she strode toward the fire. The scent of chocolate rose into the air, mingling with the musical sound of her voice, and Kyler had never been more thankful for snow in his life.

———

HE WOKE HOURS LATER, in the bottom bunk, shivering. The only warm spot on his body was a small patch on his chest, where BB lay pressed up against his body. Kyler's teeth knocked together as he scrabbled around for that spare blanket he'd brought in before the fire, the hot chocolate, and the lazy hour of conversation with a beautiful woman.

Finding the blanket, he dragged it onto himself, checking to make sure the door was still open, still able to receive the heat from the fire. The orange glow that had been present when he'd gone to bed didn't seem quite as robust, and he heaved himself out of bed. Keeping the blanket draped around his shoulders and scooping BB into one hand, he went down the hall to put on more wood and get the cabin warm again.

He glanced into Dahlia's room as he passed, but it was too dark to see anything. He'd just put the third log on the fire and started poking around to get the wood to catch the flame when she said, "I could've done that."

He spun, his heart pounding in the back of his throat. "Dahlia." She wore a dark sweatshirt and had brought out the blanket from the green room, which covered her lap. He drank in the soft, feminine shape of her face, the way she looked sleepy and sexy fresh from slumber, how she ran her hand through her hair, pushing it out of her eyes.

And stars alive, those eyes. Kyler could dive in and never surface from their dark depths.

BB jumped up on the couch to her lap, making himself comfortable. She glanced down at the little dog and giggled.

"Were you cold?" he asked, collecting his dog with an apology in his eyes. He caught sight of her gray sweat pants, and somehow the woman made such things look like high fashion.

"Oh, he's fine." She nodded and folded her arms across her middle, where BB had just been. "Maybe a little nervous too."

He turned his back to the fire, the logs he'd put on uniting with the flames just fine and pumping out the heat he wanted. He was very aware that he wore a thin T-shirt and gym shorts. He hadn't checked the weather before coming, and had never been cold in the cabin in June.

"Nervous? About what?" He stroked BB, as much to calm the dog as to soothe himself.

"This is a strange place," she said simply.

He accepted her answer, not sure what else to add to the conversation.

"Do you come out here alone very often?" she asked.

"Maybe once or twice a year." He didn't want to get too deep into his reasons, but he added, "Sometimes I just need to be by myself to...reset. Get my head back together. You know?"

Surprisingly, the woman who seemingly had everything together, always, nodded. "I completely know that, yes."

Earlier, they'd spoken about his family, the dogs he'd owned over the years, and what he used to do with his siblings up here at the cabin. Dahlia had contributed little to the conversation except to ask another question, or nod, or laugh at something he'd told her. Kyler had gone to bed kicking himself for dominating the conversation so completely, but she honestly hadn't seemed to mind.

"Your job must be stressful sometimes," he said, hoping she'd talk now.

She yawned and lay back down on the pillow she'd brought out of the bedroom with her. "It definitely can be." She smiled at him, and in the glow of the fire, it was the perfect smile. Soft, and sweet, and beautiful. His heart kicked into another gear and he couldn't help reaching out to stroke her hair off her face, tucking it behind her ear.

A shock traveled the length of his arm, from fingertip to shoulder, and her eyes widened as if she'd experienced the same electricity.

"I never did get your number," he whispered.

Her eyes closed, that dreamy smile still on her face. "I don't even have my phone with me, remember?"

"I still want to get it."

She opened her eyes and looked right at him, seemingly into his very soul. The moment lengthened, with just the crackling of the fire in the background. Kyler watched the slow rise and fall of her chest, wanting to exist inside this magical sphere for just a moment longer.

"I won't forget to give it to you," she said.

He nodded though a slip of frustration moved through him.

"Do you think we'll be able to get out of here tomorrow?" she asked, her voice barely louder than his breathing.

"Not on my bike," he said. "Maybe if the Chief sends someone for you." He wasn't sure what she'd told the person she'd called last night. She'd said she needed to call in, and she had. She'd seemed happy with the resulting conversation, and it was at that point that Kyler felt like she'd really relaxed.

"It's Saturday," she murmured. "I told Stace not to

worry about me. That we had a phone and food and all of that. They know where we are."

Relief and joy spread through Kyler. Maybe he'd get another day trapped inside the cabin with her. Maybe two or three.

"My family knows where we are too," he said. "Well, I mean, they know I'm up here. I didn't tell anyone about you."

Dahlia smiled and extended her hand toward him, her eyes still steadfastly closed. He laced his fingers through hers, leaned back against the couch, and sighed. Touching Dahlia was exhilarating, and though he'd pay for this simple gesture in the morning, right now, he let the fireworks spin and pop through him, his eyes wide open.

CHAPTER 4

The scent of bacon teased Dahlia's nose. Everything beyond her closed eyelids seemed too white, and when she opened her eyes, sure enough, she got blinded. She yawned as she sat up, her eyes squinted toward the windows and then toward the kitchen.

"Hey," Kyler said with a smile in his voice. Dahlia couldn't actually see him quite yet. "You hungry?"

Her stomach flipped at the bass notes in his voice and the thought of consuming whatever he was cooking. "Yes." She stood, the knots in her back not as bad as they'd been yesterday. "I haven't slept that good for a long time."

Glancing up from the pan, Kyler wore an inquisitive glint in his expression. "Oh yeah? On a couch in a snowed-in cabin is where you get your best sleep, huh?"

Dahlia slid onto the stool at the counter. "I usually

work late and get up early," she said, the strong lines of his face coming into focus now. He was incredibly handsome, and Dahlia wondered why she'd never noticed him before practically beating down the door of his family's cabin out in the remote hills.

"I do the early morning really well." Kyler made short work of the eggs in the pan. "Bacon, egg, and cheese sandwich? Or just bacon and eggs?"

"Sandwich."

He beamed as he pushed down the lever on a double toaster and Dahlia caught the tail end of two English muffins going in. "A woman after my own heart."

She giggled. "You're a big sandwich fan?"

"If you can put it between bread, I'll eat it." He flipped off the burner and placed a slice of cheese over the egg patties he'd made. After covering that with a lid, he finally trained a full look on her. His eyes burned with an intensity Dahlia hadn't seen many men wear, especially when they looked at her.

"Why do you work late?" he asked.

"Crime never sleeps," she said. "And the paperwork never ends." Oh, how she loathed paperwork. If someone had told her that becoming a detective for the Unified Police Force would come with so much paperwork, she wouldn't have applied so aggressively for the position.

"What kind of crimes do you deal with?" he asked. "I mean, I've never heard of anything too exciting happening in Brush Creek."

Dahlia's defenses flew into place, but she worked to

bring them back down. One of the reasons she didn't have many boyfriends was because she didn't talk about herself much. And she didn't like talking about her job at all. Some of it she *couldn't* talk about.

But as she drank in the curiosity on Kyler's face—along with the complete meekness—she found herself wanting to share a whole lot of herself with him.

"We mostly work with the farms and ranches out here," she said. "Theft, vandalism, that kind of thing. Very few cases in Brush Creek or Beaverton or Maple Mountain that the local police can't deal with. But if they need a consult or an extra pair of eyes, we do that too."

"And you've been doing it, what? Two years?"

"Just about," she said. "How did you know that?" Maybe he'd been more aware of her than she had been of him.

"You were the training officer for my brother-in-law," he said. "I mean, he wasn't my brother-in-law at the time, but he is now. Tate Benson?"

"Oh, of course. Tate and Wren." Dahlia grinned, more grateful for this easy conversation and lull in her busy life than she knew how to deal with.

The English muffins popped up and Kyler buttered them before sliding the egg and cheese onto them and crisscrossing two pieces of bacon. "Here you go, Detective."

She rolled her eyes good-naturedly. "If we go out, you can't call me that."

"*If* we go out?" He lifted his eyebrows, his own sandwich stalling halfway to his mouth.

She ducked her head, a warm glow starting in her stomach and moving upward. "When," she clarified.

"I think I should get your number now, just to be sure."

She took a bite of her sandwich, a moan starting as the salty bacon and the melty cheese met her taste buds. Kyler finally took a bite of his breakfast too, and Dahlia watched him. He seemed put out that she hadn't given him her number yet. She honestly didn't know why she was stalling. Maybe because his interest in her would melt when the snow did.

Don't be stupid, she told herself. She'd already taken a baby step by telling him a few sentences about her job. And Kyler had asked about going out with her several times.

She put her sandwich down and got up to get the pencil from where he'd left it next to the crossword puzzle book on the table. Scrawling her number in the corner, she said, "There you go. There's my number."

Their eyes met as she turned and retook her place at the bar. The heat and connection between them could've been imagined. But Dahlia knew it wasn't.

"So." Kyler cleared his throat, a ruddiness entering his neck. "I was going to go hiking and fishing today, but with the snow, I think that's going to turn into snowshoeing. You want to come with?"

"You have snowshoes here?"

He nodded and bit into his sandwich again. After swallowing, he said, "We have everything."

"Except a way back down to civilization," she pointed out.

"Well, if I'd come in my truck, that wouldn't be a problem." He shrugged and finished his sandwich. "Besides, I don't want to get back to civilization quite yet."

And dang, Dahlia didn't either, not if it meant she had to separate herself from Kyler's presence. She had no idea what to do with these new thoughts and feelings for this man, someone she'd known about for years.

"Your clothes from yesterday are dry," he said. "But I didn't see a coat or anything."

"I just had my jacket." She indicated where it hung by the front door.

"I'll see what I can rustle up."

She scanned him from head to toe. "Yeah, because you can't wear a T-shirt and gym shorts to go snowshoeing."

He blinked, the surprise in his gaze easy to find. "I didn't check the weather before coming up here."

"Obviously." She cocked her head, enjoying this game where she got to tease him. "Why is that? You go out in the wilderness and don't prepare?"

"I'm more of an open the front door and see if it's raining type of guy." He flashed her a smile. "But I'm never late. So." He shrugged those powerful shoulders.

"Can't be perfect, you know?" He stepped out of the kitchen and went through the door to her left.

She finished eating while he banged around in there, finally emerging with more winter gear than Dahlia thought possible.

"Have you ever snowshoed before?" he asked, dumping the armful of clothes on the couch and turning to her.

"Yeah, lots of times."

"Great." He started digging through the coats. "I think this one might fit." He held up a black coat with a big hood trimmed in charcoal-colored faux fur. "It was Dawn's."

Dahlia left her plate on the counter and went to take the coat from him. He held it open for her, and she couldn't look away from him as she slipped her arm into the sleeve. He pulled it around for her to put her other hand in, and somehow it was a sensual thing to do. Intimate. Like something a man would do for his wife or girlfriend.

She tugged the front closed, zipping it up easily. "Fits great." She turned and gave him her flirtiest smile. She wasn't sure quite how flirty it was, as it was a bit rusty and out of practice. "How does it look?"

"You're beautiful." His voice caught along the hard vowels, and he quickly backed up a step. But he met the couch behind him and stumbled. His arm flew out as if to find something to catch himself, and his face turned into a mask of simultaneous alarm and surprise.

Dahlia flung her hand out, and his fingers latched onto hers. But he weighed a lot more than her, and before she knew it, he'd fallen backward over the arm of the couch—and pulled her right with him.

He grunted and groaned with her body weight on top of his. She came to rest, her face stopping only a few inches from his. She could see every fleck of blue in his dark eyes, and some of them glinted with merriment. Desire. Heat. Laughter.

A laugh choked in her throat too, and she let it loose. "Sorry," she said between the giggles. "I don't know why I thought that would work."

He started laughing too, and his arms came around her, twisting her so she was on the couch and not on top of him. Dahlia felt safe, warm, in the circle of his arms, and she sobered quickly, her gaze catching on his as he quieted too.

"This isn't too weird, is it?" he whispered.

"What?" She kept her voice as soft as his.

In response, his eyes drifted closed lazily, and his lips brushed against hers. Sparks flamed in her mouth, and she pulled in a breath when he put a speck of distance between them. Dahlia felt like a teenager instead of a middle-aged woman. A sigh passed through her whole body, and her lips curled into a smile.

"Okay?" Kyler asked. "I mean—"

She pressed her mouth against his again, this time in a proper kiss that he returned as his hands came up to cradle her face.

CHAPTER 5

Kyler had lost his ever-loving mind. First from whatever had possessed him to kiss Dahlia while their legs hung over the arm of the couch. And second from how fantastic it felt to hold her in his arms and kiss her.

Just like she'd started the kiss, she ended it by tucking her face into the hollow of his throat. His pulse felt erratic in his neck, spurred on by her exhalations against his skin. He wanted to make sure he hadn't screwed anything up by kissing her less than twenty-four hours after meeting her.

Honestly, he'd met her before, but this was different.

"Okay," he finally said, a whole army of frogs in his voice. "So do we still want to go snowshoeing?"

"Yes," she said, lifting her face from his chest. "I do. Do you?"

"Absolutely." He couldn't stay cooped up in the

cabin all day. "I think we'll be able to get out the back door. The wind blows from east to west, so the front always gets the drifts."

"Have you tried going outside?"

"Not yet." He hefted himself to a sitting position on the end of the couch and stood up. "You've got a coat. Let me find one." He sifted through the pile of winter gear again, pulling out a black parka that his father had worn. It was a little too big, but Kyler zipped it up anyway. He found a pair of mittens and handed them to Dahlia.

"Boots are in the mudroom," he said. "So are the snowshoes." He grabbed a beanie and pulled it over his shorn hair before snatching a pair of gloves for himself. "It looks like the sun's out, at least." The light streaming in from the kitchen windows was promising.

Once they were properly outfitted with boots, snowshoes, and sunglasses, Kyler twisted the doorknob and said, "Moment of truth." He flashed the best smile he could, glad when Dahlia returned it with a beautiful one of her own.

He tugged on the doorknob, a blip of adrenaline shooting through him when it stuck. Then a cracking sound, like ice breaking, filled the mudroom and the door came free. He stumbled with the force he'd put behind the pull and nearly went down for a second time. Flustered, and with the heat of embarrassment in his face, he cleared his throat and straightened.

"All right. I'll go first?"

"Lead on," Dahlia said, and Kyler stepped awkwardly toward the door and looked outside. It usually took four steps to get to the ground, but with all the drifted snow, he'd only have to go down one to reach the surface.

"Poles?" He reached up and unhooked the straps from the wall beside the door.

"Sure." She accepted the pair from him, and he took another set down.

"Here we go."

The wind cut into his face the moment he stepped outside, and Kyler flipped up the hood on the coat and pulled the ties tight. He probably should've scrounged around for a scarf while he was gearing up. Too late now. Parts of him were too hot, with other parts too cold, but the snowshoes made walking easy.

Snow obliterated the landscape, but he could still easily tell where he was. "Maybe out to the creek and back?"

"Sure." Dahlia followed him for the first few yards, then she came up alongside him. "So I'm thinking I'd like to try that new restaurant in town."

"The Bread Table?" Kyler had been with Tate and Wren and a third grade teacher on a double date. The place was busy, with everyone in town trying it out—and coming back. "You haven't been?"

"It's only been open for a couple of weeks."

And Kyler hadn't been on a date since that teacher. Frustrated that there hadn't been a spark with her—with any of the last eight women he'd gone out with—he'd planned a trip to the cabin to get his bearings and figure out what to do.

"It's good," he said. "We can go tonight if we can get down the canyon."

She cut him a look, but he couldn't see her eyes through the shiny sunglasses. "I thought you were spending the weekend up here."

"I am."

"It's only Saturday."

He wanted to hold her hand, say something sweet and romantic. But nothing came to mind and his fingers were clothed in gloves.

"I can come back up after," he said.

"It's an hour-long drive. One way."

He wasn't sure if she was simply incredulous or she didn't want to put him out. "Monday night then." The restaurant would be less busy then, and Kyler wouldn't have to endure so many questions from his brothers.

"Monday should work," she said.

"It's a date." Kyler started up the hill, the climb much harder in the snow than he'd been anticipating this weekend. Dahlia kept pace with him easily, her breath hovering in the air before she moved past it.

They made it to the stream, and he handed her a bottle of water from the hip pack he wore. "Whew. Now I'm sweating." He gave her a smile and then drank.

"Can I ask you something?"

"Sure."

"Why haven't you gotten married?" She watched

him with interest in her eyes, and he felt very much like she was Dahlia the detective and he better answer truthfully.

"Who says I have to be married by now?"

"You've got to be, what? Thirty-four? Something like that."

"Thirty-five, actually."

"And you're handsome, hardworking, employed—that's a big one, you know." She ticked her finger in the air like she was checking a box. "How is it that you haven't been claimed?"

Kyler looked over the expanse of snow, his old feelings churning toward the surface. He'd thought they were gone, buried, reclaimed. But the simple thought of speaking his ex's name had his throat knotting.

"I dated someone for a long time," he said. "We were serious." The story stalled for a moment as Kyler tried to figure out how much to tell her.

All of it, he thought. He wanted her to know all of it. After all, he'd already kissed her and they had a date on the horizon, and Kyler hadn't felt a spark this hot for anyone since Katie.

"Diamond-status serious," he said. "I hadn't proposed quite yet, but we'd gone to Vernal and even Salt Lake City to look at rings." The memories flowed through him, out of him, cleansing him.

"I went to pick her up one day and found a note taped to the front door. 'I can't do this.'" Kyler looked at Dahlia and found her intense eyes staring straight at him.

"That's what the note said. Nothing more. I never heard from her or saw her again."

"You're kidding."

He gave a mirthless laugh. "I wish I was." Drawing in a deep breath, he realized that now that he'd spoken the story, it didn't seethe inside him quite so violently. "And that was it for me for a few years. She took a long time for me to get over."

"And you think you're over her now?"

Kyler took a few moments to search through his feelings. "Yeah," he said slowly. "I know I am."

She tucked her hand through his arm and leaned her head against his bicep. "Okay, then." They stood together in the snow as the sun warmed the earth, and Kyler wondered if he'd ever been this happy with Katie.

It's new, he told himself. *Don't get all carried away.* If there was another flaw to be found in Kyler, it was how easily he tended to get caught up in things. In sixth grade he'd adopted every stray cat that crossed his path after watching a video from the humane society on the fate of animals in their shelters.

He'd kept them in the barn for several weeks before his mother had found out, and then the claws came out. She'd told him his heart was so big, and she loved that about him, but they couldn't keep and feed two dozen cats.

Kyler wasn't sure why not. He'd already been doing it for a while, but he'd learned by then not to argue with his mother.

His phone rang, and he extracted it from his pocket to find an unknown number on the screen. He typically balked at answering such calls, but something told him to pick this one up.

"Hello?"

"Hello?" a man asked. "Is Dahlia there?"

Kyler tilted his chin toward her. "Yeah, she's here."

"It's her partner, Gray Salisbury. I'm at the cabin. Where are you two?"

Dahlia stepped away from Kyler like Gray might see them all cuddled up. But they'd come up a hill and back down the swell, and the cabin couldn't be seen from here. "Gray's here?"

Kyler handed her the phone, and she put it up to her ear. "Yes, I'm here. You got up the road?" She nodded, turning away from him slightly. "Yeah, sure...maybe thirty minutes...great."

She hung up and handed the phone back, her eyes bright. "My partner made it up the canyon, and he says the plows have been out and everything's melting already."

"That's great news," Kyler said, though he didn't really think so. It meant she'd be leaving soon, and he wanted to hold her hand beside the fireplace again that evening.

"I need to get back," she said. "Gray and I have work to catch up on."

"Of course." He turned with her and they began their trek back to the cabin. He felt her slipping away from him, though she chatted about her parents and how she'd once come home to find her cat on the roof.

Once they reached the cabin, Dahlia flew into Tasmanian devil mode as she gathered her clothes, disappeared down the hall to change, and came out looking authoritative and in command in her uniform, her dark hair swept back into a no-nonsense ponytail.

"He's waiting in the car," she said, edging toward the front door. "So…"

Kyler got up from where he'd been sitting on the couch, staring into the charred remains of last night's fire. "So I'll see you Monday." Hoping he wasn't being too forward or that his advances wouldn't be too awkward, he swept one arm around her waist and dipped his head to kiss her.

She seemed to melt into him, both hands going to his chest and fisting the fabric of his shirt to hold him in place close to her. She smiled to break the kiss and repeated, "Monday," before turning and opening the front door. Pausing in the doorway, she twisted back to him and said, "Thanks for everything, Kyler. Call me later, okay?"

Kyler nodded and caught the door as it swung closed and watched her slog her way through the slushy snow to the police cruiser at the end of the driveway. His bike still seemed plenty snowed in as he lifted his hand in a friendly wave and Dahlia ducked into the car with her partner.

A flash of jealousy stole through Kyler. "Don't be

like that," he muttered to himself as he retreated inside the cabin and closed the door. Though the sun was shining and hopefully the snow would be melted by afternoon, he brought in more wood and built another fire just so he could entertain himself with the joyful flames.

He knew there was nothing going on with Dahlia and Gray. They worked together, and if he didn't like her partnering up with men, he better find someone else to kiss. Because in her line of work, she'd always be paired with a male.

Staring into the flames, he prayed for clarity. Often, when he had to come to the cabin to get a reboot, it started with prayer. He hadn't really done that yet this weekend, because Dahlia had shown up within a half an hour of his arrival.

But he did now, and the pleadings to the Lord were even more complicated than they would've been the previous evening. He didn't need concrete answers, not right away. He just needed to know that he was still on the path God wanted him on.

He finished his prayers, and nothing came to his mind. Nothing he needed to correct or change. So he got up, wiped his hands down his jeans, and said, "Time for lunch," as if Dahlia was still there to talk to.

Chapter 6

Dahlia exhaled as if she'd just been through the worst ordeal of her life. Gray cast her a long look before putting the car in gear and easing it into a three-point turnabout to get them pointed in the right direction.

"You okay?" he finally asked.

She leaned her head against the headrest and let it fall in his direction. He was a couple of years older than her, married and divorced, with a thirteen-year-old daughter who lived with his mother in Maple Mountain.

Gray lived there too, making the thirty-minute drive to their offices in Beaverton every day. He sported dark hair that was starting to go gray along his sideburns and though he'd probably shaved that morning, his facial hair was already starting to grow in again. Because he spent so much time outside, he was tan year-round, even after a snowstorm.

"Fine," she said. Her stomach grumbled, and she couldn't help wondering what Kyler would be making for lunch. Something like a meatball sub, she supposed, a smile drifting across her face.

"Who was that?" Gray asked, his voice in semi-detective mode. "He looked familiar." Because Gray didn't live in Brush Creek, he wasn't as familiar with all the townspeople as Dahlia.

"Kyler Fuller," she said. "The Fullers are an original Brush Creek family."

"Lucky he was up here," Gray commented.

"I would've broken in," she said. "The hail was really coming down. Where did you take shelter?"

"I'd circled back to the cruiser already," he said, glancing at her. "I tried you on the radio for an hour."

She looked at the helpless device in her hands. "Yeah, I tried you too. It must've shorted out."

"I didn't know what else to do, and the weather was too bad to go looking on foot. Then Stace got ahold of me and said you'd found a cabin. I went home after that."

"I don't suppose you're taking me home right now?" They inched ever so slowly over the snow-covered roads. The sun had warmed everything again, making it soft and heavy with water. The further down the canyon they went, the less snow there was.

"I can, for a few minutes," he said. "We were so close."

"So we lost the trail?" They'd split up to follow the

tracks of the man they'd been looking for. Every clue had pointed them up the canyon, and when Dahlia had seen Kyler's cabin alight in the storm, she'd paused against the trunk of a tree. She hadn't known who would be on the other side of the door, and since they didn't have an actual identity of the coyote they'd been investigating, it could've been him.

"Unless it's Kyler Fuller." Gray gave her a look Dahlia recoiled from. She stiffened as she looked away.

"It's not Kyler Fuller."

"How do you know?"

"I just know." Sometimes that was true. Dahlia had been born with a detective's gut, and it was telling her that Kyler wasn't the one smuggling drugs through this remote corner of Utah. They'd been working with the big wigs in Salt Lake City, Denver, and even as far north as Boise, where the heroin and methamphetamines from Mexico were being found.

And it had all been traced back to a contact in their part of the state. They were working with a sketch artist's rendition of the man, and he'd been labeled a coyote because law enforcement believed he distributed the drugs using people who had also been smuggled across the border.

Two task forces had been in Beaverton for a pow wow a week ago, and Dahlia was a fool to think she could have more than a few minutes at home to feed her cat and brush her teeth. Even worse, she couldn't believe she'd hoped to stay at the cabin all day with Kyler.

Gray kept his focus on the road as the cruiser fishtailed a little in the sloppy snow. "It could be him."

"It's not him." Kyler was too clean-cut to be their coyote.

"We should look into his activities for the past few months anyway. I mean, why's he out here during a hailstorm?" Gray was right to be suspicious—heck, Dahlia had been too. But she'd decided her need to get out of the storm outweighed the possibility of coming face-to-face with the coyote.

"Yeah, we probably should," she agreed. "But you're just going to find out how many lawns he's mowed. He works for his family's company, A Jack of All Trades."

"My wife uses them for cleaning." Gray kept his voice light, but Dahlia had been working with him long enough to know that the gears were turning in his mind. "I'll get Val on him anyway. Just to be sure."

"Of course." Dahlia closed her eyes to relive that first kiss with Kyler, the way he'd tasted like mint and chocolate, how gentle yet demanding his mouth had been. She didn't have to tell Gray about anything she'd done at the cabin. It was none of his business. Val would check on Kyler's activities, see that he wasn't involved, and Dahlia could go to dinner with him on Monday night, no problem.

"Is my phone in here?" she asked, opening her eyes to glance around the interior of the car.

"Plugged in for you." Gray indicated her black device in the console between them.

She picked it up. "Thanks, Gray." It had been silenced, as it always was during their outdoor investigations. She'd left it behind in the car on accident, and as she swiped it open, she found half a dozen calls from Gray, two from Stace at their field office, and a single text from an unknown number.

Dahlia got a variety of texts and calls from unknown numbers—the contacts she'd collected over the years. Maybe one of them had finally come through with information that would crack this coyote case wide open.

But the message read, This is Kyler. Just texting to give you my number.

She smiled at the words, at the thought of him sitting in the cabin, texting her. The grin fell from her face when she felt the weight of Gray's eyes on her. Quickly, she saved him in her contacts and deleted the text without responding.

They finally made it to a paved, cleared road, and the trip picked up from there. With Gray waiting outside her house, Dahlia ran inside to take care of a few things. She paused just inside the doorway, her house feeling stale and joyless—the exact opposite of how the cabin had felt.

It made no sense, but Kyler's sudden introduction to her life had opened her eyes to how drab and meaningless it had become. She had functional furniture in the living room, which opened up to the kitchen behind it. Ally sat on the counter, her cat eyes glaring at Dahlia for not returning last night to feed her.

"I know," Dahlia said, striding past the couch she hardly ever sat on anymore. Since the coyote case had been brought to them six months ago, she'd spent more time at work than she did at home. And when she did come home, it was usually to crash and get as much sleep as possible before she had to face another day of unknowns, questions, theories, and fruitless hiking in circles as they looked for clues.

"We were *so close*," she told the cat, her one true confidante. "Evidence that he'd been in those woods within the last three days." She scooped the white and gray cat into her arms and opened the cupboard where she kept the cat food.

"Then the hail started. I'm sure any trace of the coyote is gone. Washed away. Frozen under snow, which will melt into a muddy mess." She refilled Ally's bowl and set it on the counter along with the cat, who started eating immediately.

As she washed out Ally's water bowl and refilled it, she said, "But I met an amazing man." The spark that had existed between her and Kyler flared to life, seeping into her voice. "And he kissed me."

She set the water bowl beside the food and absently reached up to touch her lips, just to make sure the memory was real. Startled at the way Kyler made her go soft, feel things she hadn't for years, and drift off into a daze, Dahlia blinked and let her hand fall back to her side.

He couldn't be the coyote. She hated that she even

had a decimal of doubt. Val would research him, his family, his business, and then clear him. Dahlia was sure of it. She just needed his name off the table before she allowed herself to kiss him again.

———

DAHLIA PUSHED into the house and didn't see either of her parents. "Mom?" Balancing the cake she'd picked up at the bakery with the cat carrier she'd stuffed Ally into at the last minute, unable to make the poor kitty stay home alone again, she glanced around.

Dahlia had been inside her house long enough to change on Saturday and then to sleep for a few hours before Gray knocked on her door and demanded coffee and that they leave in five minutes so they could go meet someone who'd called in about having seen their coyote.

Couldn't be a citizen, as nothing about the coyote or the drugs passing through their county had been made public. Not the sketch. Not that there was an investigation going at all.

She'd barely set the coffee when he'd knocked, and he grumbled the whole time while it brewed. Then it had been go, go, go, talk, talk, talk to people who didn't know anything, hadn't seen anything or anyone, and Dahlia was tired.

Thus, the chocolate cake she'd picked up at Sweets, the bakery on the edge of Vernal that her father had first introduced her to as a child. Some of her best memories were of her and her father riding their bikes under the clear blue sky to go fishing and stopping at Sweets on the way home for cupcakes or cookies or her personal favorite, baklava.

When her mother didn't answer, Dahlia tried, "Dad?" She always came for lunch on Sunday, and it was odd they weren't waiting for her in their favorite armchairs in the living room.

If they'd gone downstairs again, Dahlia wasn't going to be as nice as she had been last time. With her mother crossing the seventy threshold earlier in the year, Dahlia had insisted they stay on the main level of the house. The last thing she needed to deal with was a broken hip on either of her aging parents.

Their cat came around the corner, so they couldn't be too far away. Dahlia could see from the front of the house to the back, and her eyes searched the backyard through the windows as she set the cake on the kitchen counter.

Movement caught her eye, and she stepped past the dining room table and slid open the glass door that led into the yard. "Mom, there you are." Her mother sat in a lawn chair while her father stood too close to a fiery grill for Dahlia's comfort. "Hey, Dad."

He lifted a hot dog in a pair of tongs, his weather-spotted hands quaking with the force of an earthquake. "Hey, sweetheart." The hot dog fell from the tongs when her father didn't have the strength to keep them clenched.

"Can you believe it snowed only a day ago?" Her mother fanned herself like the temperature had reached triple digits. The snow had barely melted completely that morning.

"Let me, Dad." Dahlia took the tongs from her father before he dropped all the hot dogs on the ground. "How was your week? Looks like Asher came and did the lawn." She'd barely glanced at it, but it was a starting place for their conversations. From there, her mother would tell her all about her friends, their little dogs, and the new neighbors down the street.

Dahlia had perfected the art of asking others about themselves, get them talking about something they were passionate about, all in the process of doing very little speaking of her own. She'd learned the skill from her father, who was exceptional with people—or at least he had been in his younger years.

A breeze kicked up as she got the last of the meat off the grill. Dahlia switched off the flame, and said, "Let's go eat," in between her mother's story about something her sister had done at church, and herded her parents inside.

She made it through dinner without her phone sounding, but when it went off, it was Gray's ringtone—which meant serious business. Not serious business came through a text. But a phone call?

"I have to take this," she told her parents. She took a few steps away before she said, "Gray?"

"Live sighting of the coyote."

"When? Where?" She swiped her keys from the kitchen counter, a mournful glance at the chocolate cake she wouldn't be able to eat.

"This morning. A cabin up the canyon."

CHAPTER 7

Kyler found his reset button about eight o'clock on Sunday morning, when he woke to the soft silence in the cabin. It had bothered him for most of the day yesterday, after Dahlia had left, but somehow in the night, everything had come into focus.

Maybe it was his prayers. Maybe it was the fact that she'd responded to his text with enthusiasm about their date the following night. It could've been anything, and Kyler didn't much care what. He was just glad he felt like himself again.

He got up, showered, and had just dipped the first sausage roll in pancake batter when someone knocked on his door. Foolishly, his heart did a little hop, skip, and jump at the thought of it being Dahlia again.

Would he react that way every time someone knocked on this cabin door?

Grinning, he set the breakfast corndog back in the

pancake batter as BB barked. He glanced at the corgi and found him skittering around the kitchen, like he knew something Kyler didn't.

"It's fine, BB," he told the little dog and went to answer the door. Instead of a gorgeous, drenched woman on the other side, a man stood there. Several inches shorter than Kyler, but with an angry, pinched look about his face that set Kyler's defenses on high. And BB behind him barking every few seconds didn't help.

He kept the door halfway closed and filled the rest of the space with his body so the man couldn't see inside and BB wouldn't rush out. The man had a whole lot of dark hair that curled at the ends, with endless black eyes that seemed to see more than Kyler wanted them to.

"What can I help you with?" Kyler noticed the scar running from behind the man's right ear, and he suddenly felt less safe out here in the wilderness. His stomach tightened, and Kyler disliked the idea that his woods weren't safe anymore.

The man didn't speak for several long seconds, and Kyler's scalp prickled. Had he gotten lost up here? Was he hurt?

Kyler scanned the man from the top of his head to his booted feet, noticing the wear and tear on the man's dirty jeans, the traces of red dust along the top edges of his bulky work boots, and the flap of his blue flannel shirt that was torn as if it had been caught on a piece of barbed wire.

He edged back six inches, his mind running through

possible things he could use to defend himself. *Fireplace poker, his hands, the empty vase on the dining room table.* BB had quieted, and Kyler knew he was no guard dog.

He wasn't sure why exactly—maybe the scar, maybe the silence, maybe the shirt—but this man screamed dangerous.

"Do you have a phone?" The man spoke in perfect English—almost too perfect given his olive skin and his rough appearance.

"Sure." Kyler made no move to retrieve it from where he'd left it on the kitchen counter, playing his favorite station from the Internet radio app he loved.

"May I borrow it for a few minutes?" A greasy smile slid across the man's face. "No more than five minutes, I promise."

Not wanting to turn his back on the man, or invite him in, Kyler stepped back into the house, said, "Just a sec," and closed the door behind him.

Something told him to send off a quick text to Milton before letting this man use his phone, so he did. *Someone here to borrow my phone. A man. Looks rough. Call me in ten?*

Kyler sent the message and stared at the closed front door, BB cowering in the corner of the kitchen, his eyes begging Kyler not to open the door again. Kyler stepped into the dining room so he could see out the window that flanked the door, and at just the right angle, he could see the dark-haired man still standing at the door. He hadn't moved at all. Didn't glance around.

Kyler's phone chirped, and he jumped with the sound and the vibration in his palm.

Get his name, Milton had said. I'll call you in eight.

Kyler erased the message and stepped past the dining room table where he'd eaten with Dahlia just as another knock came on the door. He whipped it open. "Sorry." He laughed, the sound obviously made of nerves and air. "Couldn't find it." He extended the phone to the man. "What's your name? I've never seen you up here."

The man's fingers—complete with something dark under the nails—curled around the end of the phone. "My buddies and I were camping at the bluff and I got separated from them."

Kyler didn't release the device. "What's your name?"

"Jose Garces."

Obviously a lie, and not only because the man didn't blink, didn't put any inflection in his voice, and didn't let go of the phone.

"Okay, Jose," Kyler said, a sliver of irony at how that statement rhymed snaking through him. He released the phone, and Jose backed up. He turned at the edge of the porch and went down the stairs, his head bent.

Kyler kept his eye on the man, first noticing more tears along the back of the man's shirt, one of the edges obviously stained with blood. He gripped the door and wished he had his phone so he could take a picture, call Milton—or better yet, the police. Why, he had no idea.

Jose wasn't trespassing; he'd come right to the front door. He hadn't done anything that Kyler knew of, other than look like he had no soul. He trailed his fingers along the seat of Kyler's motorcycle, his back still the only view Kyler had. He froze, wondering if this man would throw his leg over the bike and take off with the two most essential things Kyler needed to survive up here.

Then his head lifted and the hand holding the phone dropped. He turned back and approached again, his stride sure and every step intimidating. At the top of the stairs, he extended the phone. "Thank you."

Kyler took it and shoved it in his back pocket. "Sure. Do you need help?"

"No, I am fine." He flashed a smile that contained no assurance, no happiness. "Do you come to this cabin often?"

"Yes," Kyler said, though he and his family really didn't use it all that often now that they were older and a lot of them were married. "My family owns it and we come all the time."

The man cocked his head as if he too could tell a lie when he heard one, nodded once, and turned away. He walked down the steps, down the driveway, and on down the road, never once looking back.

Kyler watched him until the top of his head disappeared down the swell in the land, only then taking a truly deep breath. His phone rang, and he nearly fell over. He darted back inside the cabin, closed and locked the door, and answered the call from Milt.

"So you're still alive?" His brother didn't sound like he was kidding, but Kyler felt like a fool.

"I'm sure he wouldn't have hurt me," he said, though he absolutely wasn't sure of that. He stepped over to the window and stared out of it, almost expecting Jose to return with a gang of similarly dirty men—his camping buddies—and burn the cabin to the ground. "He said his name was Jose Garces and that he was camping with his buddies at the bluffs."

"And he wanted what?"

"He needed to use my phone."

"Who did he call?"

"I didn't ask him."

"Look at the number."

Why Milton was so interested, Kyler wasn't sure. And what would he do? Call the same number? Kyler *really* didn't think that was a good idea. But he said, "All right, hold on," and put his brother on speaker so he could navigate to his call history.

He repeated the number to Milt and scanned the front of the cabin again. No movement. No one. He still felt too exposed out here, and he decided to leave earlier than planned.

"I'm talking to Tate about it," Milt said. "He doesn't want you to worry, but I think you should come down to town."

"He went off in the wrong direction," Kyler said, his voice in a monotone.

"What?"

"The man. Jose. Whoever. He said he was camping with his buddies at the bluffs, but when he left, he went straight down the road. The bluffs are to the west." He looked in the direction Jose should've gone, but nothing seemed out of place.

"And he asked me if we come up here and use this cabin much."

"What did you tell him?"

"I said we were up here all the time." Kyler turned away from the window and went back into the kitchen. He turned off the stove where the oil he'd been heating was probably now scorched. "I'm cleaning up and coming back," he said. "It'll probably take me a couple of hours to get everything done here and back to Brush Creek."

"Keep me updated," Milt said. "I want to know when you leave, anything you see or hear."

Kyler nodded and said, "Okay," when he remembered his brother couldn't see him. He hung up and launched himself into full clean-up mode, desperation driving him to get out of the canyon as soon as possible.

———

NINETY MINUTES LATER, he had everything scrubbed and put away in the cabin, his backpack packed and lying next to the front door, and BB secure in his kennel that strapped to the back of Kyler's bike. He'd closed all the blinds and made sure the back door leading to the mudroom was tightly locked and then the chain hooked into place. They had had some break-ins in the past, but nothing nefarious. Stranded hikers or campers in a bad storm, like Dahlia had been.

For some reason, Kyler hadn't called or texted her about the incident with Jose. She hadn't answered any of his questions about what she'd been doing or investigating on Friday night, and Milt had assured him that Tate was learning what he could.

It probably wasn't anything. A guy who needed to make a phone call. That wasn't a crime, and neither was walking around in dirty jeans and a torn shirt.

Leaving now, he typed out, almost smashing his thumb against the send button in his over-anxious state.

He picked up his pack and swung it onto his back, pulling open the door with one hand while digging in his jeans pocket for the keys with the other. His father had always warned him to lock the cabin tight, and Kyler didn't think there was a more crucial time to follow those directions.

With the lock in place, and the deadbolt too, Kyler reached for the helmet he'd left on the long, wide railing that fenced in the porch. Tires popped over gravel, and his heart started shooting around in his chest like a ball of fireworks.

A police car came into view, but it was unlike the one Dahlia had climbed into yesterday morning. This one belonged to McDermott Boyd, and the man himself climbed out of the front seat, taking several seconds to drink in the scenery before him.

"McDermott?" Kyler asked, hurrying toward the steps. "What's going on?"

"Stop!" McDermott held up his hand, and Kyler froze. His best friend strode forward, his eyes tense and anxious. "Have you been down the steps yet?"

"No."

"I got wind that you'd met a man up here," he said, stopping a good distance back. "We're interested in collecting evidence if we can find it. We need you to stay right where you are."

Another car rolled up, this one a cruiser from the Beaverton Police Department.

"Evidence?" Kyler repeated. "Evidence of what?"

McDermott studied the ground. "Footprints. Dust, hair, fibers, anything."

"Who was that guy?" Kyler asked.

"We don't know." McDermott took another step; he was almost to the motorcycle.

"He touched that," Kyler blurted out. McDermott's head popped up, his eyes wide. "The bike," Kyler continued. "He touched it. Ran his finger along the seat. Stood right next to it. Walked from here to there, and then back. He had his hands all over my phone too."

Kyler took it out of his pocket, sure he'd erased the evidence the police needed. "It's been in and out of my pocket, and I've touched it a lot too."

"Set it on the railing there," he said. "The helmet too." McDermott nodded when Kyler followed his directions. "Step to the side, Kyler. The detectives will be here to question you in a few minutes." He smiled, and it was the same kind, brotherly smile Kyler had always seen on McDermott's face.

"Am I in trouble?" he called to his friend as he turned to the pair of Beaverton cops that had joined him.

"No, Kyler," McDermott assured him. "You'll be fine."

Fine wasn't the same as *not in trouble*, but Kyler stepped to the side and set his heavy backpack on the porch. And when that same car pulled up and Gray and Dahlia got out, they both looked grim, fierce, and absolutely like he was in seriously big trouble.

Dahlia had been praying for a solid hour by the time she pulled up to Kyler's cabin. Just for good measure she sent another prayer heavenward. *Please let him be innocent.*

He was the first man who'd got her pulse doing more than a gentle lope in years. Why did he have to be involved with the coyote?

"I'll start," Gray murmured, his mirrored shades barely turning her direction. Why he was telling her, she didn't know. Gray always started with their witnesses. Dahlia was the observer, and she could peg lies and omissions nine-and-a-half times out of ten.

They paused at the handlebars of the bike to check in with McDermott Boyd, the state trooper in this county. He alone out of the other police forces in the Brush Creek area knew of the coyote. "He's a friend of yours, right?" Gray asked.

"From childhood," McDermott said, glancing toward Kyler. "He said the coyote touched his motorcycle. I've got a crime scene team coming from Vernal. They're thirty minutes out."

"What else?" Dahlia surveyed the scene, but there was too much going on for her to take in specific details.

"His phone, which he set on the railing there. He said the coyote walked to the door, knocked twice, down the steps, touched the bike, and back."

Dahlia couldn't look away from Kyler, but she kept her ear solidly on the conversation. "He looks scared."

"He is," McDermott said. "But I don't think he's involved in any way. A chance encounter."

"Our biggest witness yet, though," Gray said. "The coyote hasn't ever approached houses before."

"Must've been desperate," Dahlia said, finally tearing her eyes from Kyler's. They called to her, even across this distance, and she kept her fists clenched in her pockets so she wouldn't disturb the crime scene by running to him.

"Can we get him down from there?" she asked. "Maybe he can go over the side."

"That's a twelve-foot drop," Gray said, nodding to the porch. "Eight steps up."

"Kyler's athletic," she said.

"The coyote could've tried the back door, gone around the side, been anywhere," McDermott said. "How crucial is it that you speak to him?"

"Beyond dire," Gray said, and Dahlia agreed. "He saw the coyote only two hours ago. He can't have gotten that far, and we need to know where he went." He stepped to the west, clearly intending to give the most crucial crime scene areas a wide berth.

Dahlia followed him around the tree where the yellow tape had been wrapped and they walked along the edge of the lawn where it turned into wild grasses.

"Is there another way down?" Gray called to Kyler. "Without going back into the house, or going down the steps there."

"No, sir," he said.

"Maybe we could talk from here." They stood about fifteen feet back from the porch, way over on the side. Gray looked at Dahlia, and she shook her head. No, this wouldn't work. She couldn't see Kyler's hands, his feet, what they did or didn't do.

"Can you come over the side, Kyler?" she asked, her chest tightening as she said his name. Why had this happened to him? She hoped her emotions and soft feelings for him wouldn't color her ability to do her job.

"I can try." He tested his weight on his hands, like he didn't believe the wide porch railing would hold him. Of course it did, and he vaulted over it, twisting to grab onto it with his hands as he dangled himself over the side.

"It's just about five more feet," Gray said. "Just drop straight down."

He did, landing with a soft grunt before turning and dusting his hands off. Walking toward them, his dark blue eyes stormed with emotion and he couldn't seem to look away from Dahlia.

Gray cleared his throat, obviously noticing. Thankfully, he didn't say anything about the electricity between Kyler and Dahlia. "Let's talk near the cruiser," he said. He went first, and Dahlia indicated that Kyler should follow Gray and she'd take up the rear.

Kyler's hand brushed hers as he passed, and Dahlia's heart tippity-tapped in her chest.

Back at the car, Gray leaned his weight against the trunk and folded his arms and crossed his ankles like he was waiting for a bus. "Tell us what happened, if you will, please." He hitched his glasses down so his bright blue eyes could be seen. "Everything, Mister Fuller. Even if you think it's not an important detail."

Kyler's fingers went round and round each other. He was nervous. He cleared his throat and cut a glance at Dahlia. "So I was making breakfast when someone knocked on the door."

"What kind of knock?" Gray asked.

"Kind of knock?" Confusion ran across Kyler's face.

"Yeah, were they pounding? How many times did they knock? Did it sound urgent? Just a knock? What kind of knock?"

"Oh, uh, just a knock," Kyler said, cutting a look at Dahlia. "When Dahlia showed up on Friday night, that was a like a frantic pounding, and I knew she was in trouble. Or whoever it was. I obviously didn't know it was her."

Dahlia wanted to smile at him, soothe him, remind him that he wasn't in any trouble. At least not yet. She simply continued to look at him, hoping he'd take some of her calm energy and use it.

"So just a knock," Gray said, his attention singular on Kyler.

"Right. So I answered the door. There was a man standing there."

"What was he wearing?"

Kyler described the work boots, the blue flannel shirt, how it was ripped on the hem and along the back. "Like he'd crawled through barbed wire," he said. "And his jeans were dirty, frayed along the bottom. His boots had the red dust on them from the bluff. He told me he had gotten separated from his friends while they were camping. He asked to use my phone."

"And you let him?"

"Yes, sir. He gave me the creeps, what with that scar on his neck, and those eyes...." He shivered. "I texted my brother that some guy had shown up and that I needed him to call me in a few minutes."

Dahlia knew the type of eyes Kyler was describing. Soulless. Endless. Seemingly omniscient. "Tell us about the scar," she said. The sketch they'd been using had been well, sketchy, in that area, as the witness who'd worked with the artist hadn't gotten a good look at that side of the coyote's body.

"It was on his right side," Kyler said. "It looked old, like something he'd had for a while. He was several inches shorter than me, so I was looking down on him, and the scar ran out from behind his ear, like this." He lifted his finger to his neck and drew in a diagonal line down toward his throat.

"Was it thick? Thin?" Dahlia asked.

"Thick near his ear, and it tapered out," Kyler said. "Went about halfway down. I remember that it was what scared me, made me feel unsafe."

Gray asked more questions, and Kyler relaxed, telling the tale of his brief yet so significant altercation with their coyote. It had definitely been him—Jose Garces as he'd told Kyler. She'd have Stace run the name, but she wasn't hopeful they'd get anything back.

The crime scene unit showed up, and they began swabbing the motorcycle for fingerprints, taking pictures of footprints, sweeping for fibers, hair, debris, or prints from the gravel driveway all the way to the front door. One of them picked up Kyler's phone with gloved hands and dropped it into a plastic evidence bag.

"We need a team out at the bluffs," Gray said when Kyler had finished. "And Stace on about half a dozen things, from the stores who carry the type of boots he was wearing to the name Jose Garces to this phone number he called."

Gray exhaled, and Dahlia knew exactly how he felt. Neither of them were wearing their official uniforms, because it was Sunday. Pretty much the only day they had off, and they'd already worked half of it that morning.

"What about my phone?" Kyler asked. "That's just gone, isn't it?"

"And the backpack, I'm afraid," Dahlia said as she watched a crime scene officer pick it up and gently place it in a paper bag.

"He didn't touch anything in that," Kyler said.

"I'll buy you a new crossword puzzle book." She tossed him a weary smile, knowing what she had to do and not wanting to do it. But this case had just been blown wide open—a live sighting of the coyote! Right here. Only hours ago—and she'd be working around the clock.

"This is locked," someone called, and Dahlia looked at Kyler.

"Do you have the keys?"

He fished them from his pocket and handed them to Gray, who passed them to another officer.

"What are they doing?"

"Everything they can to figure out who this guy is," Gray said. "They'll go inside and around the entire property outside too." He watched them for a moment. "They won't touch anything."

"I cleaned up inside," Kyler said. "Laundry, dishes, bathroom, all of it." He looked sheepish. "My mother doesn't like it when the cabin is left a mess."

"The coyote didn't go inside," Gray said. "I'm sure—"

"The coyote?" Kyler's worried gaze flew from Gray to Dahlia. "That's what you're calling him? What does he do? Smuggle people through small towns in Utah?"

Gray winced, realizing his mistake. "We don't know

everything he does," he said tactfully. "That's why we're trying to find him."

Kyler cocked his hip, clearly not believing Gray. "Dahlia," he said, and though his voice didn't go up in inflection, he was still asking her a question.

"I can't talk about it, Kyler," she said, wishing she could. Maybe she'd be able to sleep better at night. Or go a single afternoon without rushing off to interrogate a witness.

"The boys from Beaverton can give you a ride down to town," McDermott said, stepping over to their conversation. "I've got a CSI team going to the bluffs." He nodded at Dahlia and then Gray before moving away again.

"I'll call in what we need Stace to get working on." Gray stepped away, his phone already on his ear, leaving Dahlia with Kyler.

She looked up at him, almost falling right over the edge of professional and into the ocean-blue eyes. "This is a major case," she said softly. "We've been working it for six months. I'm sorry, Kyler. I can't tell you much else." She wanted to reach out and touch him but not in mixed company.

Too bad he didn't seem to care about that. He let his hand feather across hers again, and she sucked in a breath and pocketed her hands. She didn't want to hurt him. She just had lines that couldn't be crossed at certain times.

She leaned in closer, and kept her voice low when she

said, "And I'll need a rain check on dinner tomorrow night. This will keep us hopping for a few days."

His face fell, and Dahlia's heart squeezed. "I'll call you later."

"I don't have a phone." He looked away, clearly frustrated and not hiding it well. Kyler didn't hide much very well, and gratitude flowed through Dahlia at that. Because he was indeed innocent. In the wrong place at the wrong time for a chance encounter with the man she'd been tracking for six months.

Maybe he'd been in the right place at the right time.

"How late is too late to stop by?" she asked.

His gaze flew back to hers, the hope there bright and beautiful. "It's never too late."

"Great, I'll see you later." She stepped away, the motion taking every ounce of willpower she had. She wanted to kiss him goodbye so he wouldn't be too disappointed about her breaking their date, but she couldn't. Not out here in the open where anyone could see.

As she joined Gray and asked, "Should one of us go out to the bluffs?" she wondered why she was so embarrassed about her relationship with Kyler.

Maybe embarrassed wasn't the right word. Maybe she just didn't want to admit the depth of her feelings for a man she'd met two days ago—in front of his best friend and her partner. So she held onto her emotions, determined to release them once she could be alone with Kyler that night.

CHAPTER 9

By the time Kyler got back to Brush Creek, he was cranky and hungrier than he'd ever been. Milt met him just inside the front door, his eyes broadcasting his worry and his relief at the same time.

"There you are."

"They took my phone."

"McDermott told me." Milt grabbed his wallet. "Let's go get a burger and a new phone."

"It's Sunday."

"A burger then." He opened the door, obviously not going to take no for an answer. "I know you're hungry."

And Kyler didn't really want to be alone either. Left to himself to consider that the man that had come to the cabin door had warranted two dozen people to come sweep for hair, fibers, take casts of his footprints, all of it. He wished now more than anything that he'd been able to take a picture of him. It seemed like Dahlia and her partner had never seen the man in real life or in a photograph.

So Kyler followed his brother out to his truck and got in, a long sigh slipping through his lips. "What a morning."

"I didn't realize how big of a deal it was," Milt said. "I was talking to Tate at his desk, and McDermott overheard me. He sort of went nuts and started asking all kinds of questions. Then he got on the phone and disappeared into his office. Next thing I know, he's dashing out and asking if I could call you to make sure you stayed at the cabin." Milt gave him a sideways glance as he drove.

They arrived at the T-junction, with Oxbow Park straight in front of them, and their destination on the other side of the forest. In the winter, Kyler could see Ruby's through the bare branches, but in mid-June, the diner was obscured.

"I didn't get a call from you," Kyler said.

"It went to voicemail."

"He must've had me put the phone down already."

Milt drove over the river and around the park, taking a spot right in front of Ruby's Roost. "Come on. Come tell me all about it." He smiled at Kyler and a blast of reassurance hit him in the chest.

"I have something else to tell you too," he said, climbing out of the truck.

"Oh yeah?" Milt kept his eye on him as Kyler circled the hood. "What about?"

"A woman."

Milt's face exploded into a smile. "How long have you been keepin' this a secret?"

Kyler shrugged. "Not that long. I met her this weekend."

His brother's smile faltered and confusion colored his face. "Weren't you at the cabin this weekend?"

"Yep." Kyler popped the P sound as he reached for the door to let himself into the diner. "And there was a storm, and this woman showed up on my doorstep needing a place to stay."

"Kyler," Milt said, a note of chastisement in his voice.

"What?" He held up two fingers to the hostess and started after her when she grabbed two menus and headed down the aisle between the tables.

"So who was she?" Milt asked as he slid into the booth across from Kyler.

"Dahlia Reid."

Milt dropped his menu. "The detective."

"The one and the same." Kyler lifted his eyes to the waitress and said, "As much Dr. Pepper as you've got. With lemon."

Milt could barely order his diet soda, and when the waitress walked away, he stared at Kyler. "I need details, now."

Warmth finally started to spread through Kyler again, and he didn't feel one breath away from shattering. "So I was just making dinner when someone pounded on the door...."

———

KYLER'S HOUSE sat in the middle of the block, on the east side of town, in a quiet neighborhood where children rode their bikes and the summer breeze lilted through the treetops. He sat on his front porch as the community went to sleep, moving to the back where there wasn't as much light pollution so he could see the stars better.

Nine o'clock came, then ten, and Dahlia didn't arrive. He could hardly stand to think of her out in the wilderness surrounding the cabin in this darkness, especially with the level of exhaustion he'd seen in her face much earlier in the day.

He wondered if this was her reality all the time, or if big cases like this were rare. He wasn't sure, but he wanted to find out. His feelings ping-ponged around, never really settling in one place long enough for him to make sense of.

When eleven o'clock hit, he went inside and brushed his teeth, BB at his heels. "She said she'd come," he told his dog, but BB just cocked his head to the side. He couldn't bring himself to commit fully to going to bed, so he stretched out on the couch, the TV on in front of him and his dog pressed against his chest. That way, he'd be closer to the front door if Dahlia came knocking.

It would normally be this time of night where Wren would text him his schedule for the following day. Milt said he'd pick him up and make sure he knew which jobs needed to be done. Kyler sighed just thinking about ten hours of trimming, weeding, hauling, and mowing. He loved it; he wasn't like Brennan who wanted to do something different with his life.

He just wanted more to his life than mowing grass or building retaining walls. He wanted someone to come home to at night, someone to share his life with besides a twenty-pound dog, maybe a few kids. Yawning, he let his eyes close, and the next time they opened, five sharp raps echoed through his still-soft mind.

His heart catapulted to the back of his throat, BB barked and jumped down from the couch, and Kyler sat up abruptly, trying to gain his bearings. The TV still flickered, as did the lamp on the end table. The knocking came again, and Kyler launched himself off the couch and to the door, saying, "Dahlia," before he even had the door open all the way.

She stood on his front porch, haloed by the light. When she looked up at him, he saw her with every defense down. She was soft and beautiful, as well as fierce and determined when she stepped into his personal space and ran her hands up his chest.

He went with her, not quite sure what she needed but willing to give it to her. Her fingers curled around the back of his neck, drawing his forehead to hers. "I'm so tired," she whispered. "And yet I couldn't just go home without seeing you."

She gave him a bit of breathing room, and their eyes

met, locked. "Why is that? I used to go home without seeing you all the time."

"Things change," he said, pushing BB back with his foot. Apparently the little dog liked Dahlia as much as Kyler did, as he kept putting his front paws on her legs.

"In an instant."

"Did you find what you were looking for up the canyon?"

Instead of answering him, she drew his mouth toward hers, kissing him with those soft lips, her fingernails tracing along his hairline and sending shivers across his shoulders. He kissed her back, exploring gently, before realizing they stood on his front porch where anyone could see.

"You want to come in?" he asked.

She nodded and stepped past him.

"Coffee?" He shut the door as BB trotted after Dahlia. "Tea? I have both."

"Tea would be great."

Kyler busied himself in the kitchen while she sank onto the couch where he'd just been asleep. One glance at the clock—twelve-ten—told him he was going to be in serious trouble tomorrow when he had to work.

A few minutes later, he presented her with a cup of chamomile, and she breathed in the steam. A smile pulled at the corners of her mouth, but it disappeared quickly. She took one sip of the tea and set the cup beside the lamp.

"Kyler, there are...certain things I can't tell you." She

kept her focus on her hands for a moment before lifting them to meet his. "Ever. Certain parts of my job that you can't know."

"All right."

"No, it's not all right."

Kyler didn't know what she expected him to say. She sighed and took his hand in hers, gently tapping it against her thigh before wrapping her other hand around his too. "You really think you can live with not knowing everything I do at work?"

She seemed genuinely concerned, and Kyler cocked his head, trying to figure out the real conversation they were having. "I don't think I need to know everything, no," he said. "I don't detail every aspect of what I do at work."

"What do you need?"

He wished he'd had a little more time to prepare to answer these questions. But he said, "I think I need to know you're safe," and that idea felt right coming from his mouth. "And that you'll be coming home at night." Vulnerability tore through him. "I think that's what I need."

"I can work on giving you those things," she said. "I've been single for so long, I sometimes forget I should check in with my boyfriends."

The word ripped through Kyler, making his blood pump faster in his veins. "Is that why you're not seeing anyone? I mean, besides me." He tried a smile, glad when her lips up curved for a moment.

"My job has ended several relationships over the years," she said. "My mother took care of the rest."

"Your mother?"

"She's a bit critical of the men I've brought home."

"How many men is that?"

"Four or five." Dahlia shrugged, her eyes trained on their joined hands. "Nothing ever worked out."

A lump formed in Kyler's throat. "Do you think we'll work out?"

Her smile carved its way across her face at the same rate it carved into his heart. "I guess we'll see," she said.

"So I'm stuck waiting for a date with the detective, is that it?" Kyler teased.

She touched her lips to his, a quick peck that still ignited something inside him he hadn't expected to ever feel again. "That's about it, yes." She stood, removing her hands from his. "I'll call you tomorrow, okay?"

"I don't have a phone, remember?" He got up and ripped off a corner from a utility bill stuck to his refrigerator. "Write your number down again, and when I get a new phone, I'll text you."

"Always trying to get my number." She giggled, wrote her number down, and gave him one more bone-melting kiss before slipping out the front door like a thief in the night.

And she really was a thief, because she'd stolen his heart after only a few days.

CHAPTER 10

The next several days passed in a blur for Dahlia. Coffee, work, stress, eat, sleep, coffee. She was never sure where her next hour would take her, and she'd been all over Maple Mountain, the bluffs, Beaverton, and the canyon where Kyler's cabin sat.

She never wanted to go to that canyon again.

The coyote had disappeared, seemingly without a trace.

Stace had searched for the number, and it belonged to a burner cell phone Dahlia and Gray found in pieces on the side of the road, only a mile from the turnoff to go up to the cabin. He'd clearly called for a pick-up, and by the time anyone knew he'd made contact with Kyler, the coyote was gone.

But who had picked him up?

Gray firmly believed their chauffeur—as they'd started calling the driver—lived nearby. How else could he or she just drop everything and get to that stretch of highway so far from civilization before McDermott Boyd arrived only ninety minutes later?

Dahlia agreed with him, but short of going door-to-door and asking, the trail had gone cold.

The fingerprints hadn't matched any in their database. The boot prints had been narrowed to two stores within a hundred-mile radius, one of which was the sporting goods store in Vernal. Dahlia and Gray had made the visit, found the boots, and questioned every employee to find out if the coyote had ever been there to buy those work boots.

Not a single person had seen him.

"He has a circle," Dahlia had told Gray when they'd left. "He doesn't go buy his own boots."

Gray's stormy expression over the top of the car said he agreed. He agreed, but he didn't like it.

Dahlia didn't either. It wasn't healthy to live, sleep, and breathe a case like this, and yet she couldn't seem to let it go. She stopped by Kyler's when she got off work before ten p.m. Otherwise, she texted him. They still hadn't gone on their date, and while he was being patient and chill about the whole thing, Dahlia feared he'd move on. Decide he didn't want to be left home alone while she ran around trying to find ghosts in the wilderness. Find another woman to talk with, hold hands at a decent hour with, and kiss goodnight.

With another Monday dawning, Dahlia stood in the shower, determined to make that evening their first official date. With damp hair and a towel still around her, she texted Gray and said she needed to take a step back from this coyote thing.

He agreed instantly, followed with Why don't you just come in this morning? I'll get TJ to go out with me if something comes up.

TJ was the Beaverton Sheriff, and he often was privy to their cases, as they shared office space with the Beaverton PD.

Take the whole afternoon off?

Sure, Gray messaged. Go get your hair done, or take a nap, or sip that fruity soda you like in the park. It's a gorgeous day.

Dahlia fingered the ends of her hair. She hadn't been to get her hair done in a while. And she did like her peach-flavored sodas. And nothing sounded more heavenly than a nap.

Except a date with Kyler.

She dressed quickly, throwing her hair into a ponytail and grabbing a banana before she left the house. Once at the office, she sat in the car and texted Kyler at his new number. *Are you free tonight? I've just decided to take the afternoon off, and we could go to dinner...*

When he didn't respond instantly, she grabbed her purse and headed into her desk. Gray already sat at his—he seemed to always arrive before Dahlia and leave after her—and he glanced up as she set her bag down, quickly followed by the forty-four-ounce soda she'd bought on the way out of town.

"Morning," she said, sitting down and jiggling her mouse to wake her computer. "Did you go home last night?"

Dahlia had managed to zip over to Vernal for a single hour to have lunch with her parents. Her father knew she was working a difficult case, and neither of her parents had said anything about her shorter and shorter visits.

"Yeah." Gray wiped both hands down his face, his eyes bleary and bloodshot when he opened them again.

"That's not healthy," Dahlia said. "You need more to your life than this job."

"Says the woman who hardly ever goes home herself."

"I'm taking the whole afternoon off."

"Which means I can't."

"Take tomorrow," she said, peeling her banana and keeping one eye on Gray. He'd been good to her, kind, patient as she learned her new role when she'd first started.

Gray sighed, a long hiss that alerted Dahlia to something more than just being overworked. "And do what?" he asked.

"Rest," she said. "Go play golf. You're always talking about that course you want to play, and you never go." She bit into her banana, fully staring at him now.

She saw him roll his eyes. Saw the tick of the muscle in his jaw. Saw the way he glanced away from her as if he had something he wanted to stay secret.

"Get a coffee," she said. "And drink it on the couch

instead of in your car. Go to breakfast with your daughter. Take a walk on the riverwalk. There are literally a hundred things you could do."

He pinned her with his detective's glare. "I could say the same for you."

"I'm taking the afternoon off," she repeated.

"You gonna finally go out with that boyfriend of yours?"

Dahlia's hand froze, her fingertips digging into the soft flesh of the banana a little too hard. "I don't have a boyfriend," she said, her eyes narrowing. "Where did you hear that?"

"That man at the cabin?" Gray said, making it a question when he already knew. "I know you like him."

Dahlia lifted her chin a fraction of an inch, refusing to confirm or deny. Surely Gray couldn't know about the kissing. Or that she'd gone to see Kyler several times last week.

"I heard something in your voice when I mentioned we should have Stace check him out."

"He checked out," Dahlia said. "And it's not his fault he was at the cabin when the coyote came. He has nothing to do with him."

Gray chuckled. "There it is again."

"There's what?" Dahlia tossed the half-eaten banana in the trash can, unable to take another bite. She didn't like mushy fruit, and she'd practically squeezed the life from the banana during this line of questioning.

"Defensiveness. And you haven't denied or

confirmed anything. Classic avoidance." Gray cocked one eyebrow at her and returned his attention to the paperwork he'd been studying. "You should go to Teddy's in Maple Mountain," he said as if she'd asked for the best restaurants for first dates.

Her phone buzzed, and she flipped it over fast just in case it was Kyler.

Gray chuckled now, and added, "They have the best burgers and sandwiches in the county."

"I'm more of a salad girl," she said.

"Right," Gray said. "But I imagine someone who works outside all day has an appetite for something more substantial in the evening." He said it casually and kept his focus on the folder, though there was no way he was even reading the report inside.

Kyler did like sandwiches, and Dahlia liked trying new places. She'd been everywhere in Brush Creek, and maybe they could make the twenty-minute drive north and experience something different.

She picked up her phone and found that Kyler had responded with *Sure! What time? Where do you want to go?*

The smile crept across her face before she could command her lips to stay straight. Of course, Gray saw it, another chuckle filling the silence between them. As Dahlia tapped out the words *I've heard Teddy's in Maple Mountain has the most amazing sandwiches and burgers,* she said to Gray, "You're a real pain, you know that?"

"Tell your boyfriend hi," he said.

Dahlia hit send on her message and looked into her partner's eyes. "I will."

———

FRESH FROM A NAP, and with hair four inches shorter, Dahlia slipped on a pair of sandals she hadn't worn since last summer. The gold straps crisscrossed over the top of her foot, and she buckled them just as Kyler knocked on her front door.

"Hey there," she said when she opened the door.

"Hey yourself." He swept into her house, right into her personal space, and kissed her. Giddy with excitement and feeling more like herself than she had in months, she giggled and kissed him back.

"A real date," he said, pulling away but keeping her in his arms. "You know, I wasn't sure this would ever happen."

Dahlia's joy dampened, and she looked into his pretty eyes. "My work isn't always this intense." She smoothed down the collar on his red polo and asked, "Should we go?"

"Yeah, let's go." He wore a pair of jeans that seemed the same hue as his eyes, and Dahlia hoped she hadn't dressed up too much. Her black shorts went down halfway to her knee, and she'd paired them with a blue tank top with a huge gold star in the center of it. Thus, the gold sandals completed the summery date look.

"You look fantastic," he murmured as he captured

her hand in his and led her down the front steps. "And I found your house easy-peasy."

She lived in one of the oldest neighborhoods in Brush Creek, with narrow streets and squatty houses in a neat row. But there was only one road into the neighborhood, and it was right off the river.

"Thank you," she said, beaming up at him as he opened the passenger door to his truck and waited for her to get in. "For waiting for me too," she added, not sure why she'd spoken.

A measure of confusion ran through his eyes. "Waiting for you?"

"Waiting for this date," she said with a little shrug, not wanting to make something that wasn't a big deal into something that was.

"You're worth the wait, Dahlia," he said, his voice real low, barely leaving his throat. He bent down and touched his lips to her forehead, sliding lower to her cheek, and then fully placing a kiss on her lips.

She breathed him in like he was pure oxygen and she was drowning. Just when the kiss was about to turn scandalous, Kyler pulled away. "Okay, wow," he said. "We should go." He left her standing next to the open door, and she climbed into the truck while he circled it.

"Sorry," he said as he started the car and adjusted the air conditioning. "That was...well, my mother wouldn't approve of kissing like that." He glanced at her, a wicked smile on his face. "I think we're consenting adults, but we should probably...." He trailed off, obviously unsure of how to finish.

"Go slow," Dahlia supplied. "Take our time. Get to know each other."

"Yeah." He put the truck in gear and backed out of her narrow driveway. "All of that."

"Can I sit by you?" she asked, the distance between them just a little too far for her. She wasn't sure why her feelings for Kyler had developed so quickly, but she didn't want to obsess over it either. She liked him; he liked her. They kissed. It was normal.

"Of course, sweetheart." He patted the seat directly next to him, and Dahlia slid over so her leg was flush with his. After taking his hand in hers, she directed him toward Teddy's, and then asked him what his role was in his family's business.

CHAPTER 11

Teddy's was clearly the place to be in Maple Mountain. Even though it was only Monday, parked cars took up the entire parking lot and had started to creep down the road in both directions.

The building sat really close to the road, out on the highway that was entering Maple Mountain, and though Kyler came this way often, he'd never stopped to find out what this old barn-like building was.

There was no sign, and he almost kept driving when Dahlia said, "I think this is it."

Their earlier kiss burned in his mind. Wow, he liked her. A lot more than he'd even thought. He liked her strength. Her work ethic, even if it did keep them apart until later in the evening. He liked her beauty, and the way she held his hand like she needed him to keep her grounded. And the way she kissed him...it was like she couldn't get enough, like if she didn't have him, she couldn't keep breathing.

Kyler liked a whole lot about her, including that even though she was a tough detective, she still made him feel like he was the one protecting her. The one lending her his strength.

"Nowhere down there," she said, scanning a row of parking out her side of the truck.

"I think we're going to have to park on the street," he said. He pulled out of the lot and continued past the brown barn with double-wide white doors. "And that place doesn't look that big. Are we sure we want to go here?"

"I've got nothin' else to do," she said. "And Gray said this place has the best sandwiches in the county. And you love sandwiches." Her fingers on his tightened. "We can wait, right?

Kyler could do a lot of things with Dahlia at his side, so he said, "Sure," and kept driving until he came to the end of the parked cars. He pulled in beside a red sedan and got out, towing Dahlia with him out his door. They made the walk back to the restaurant hand-in-hand while he contemplated asking her about a more sensitive subject.

"So," he said. "You know about my family. I know about yours. I've blathered on long enough about my job. You don't really talk about yours." He paused at the doorway, one hand on the long handle. "What about church? Do you go?"

He opened the door and a wall of noise hit him. The country music coming from the place could make a deaf man cringe, and while Kyler wanted to sample the sandwiches, he also wanted a more intimate date with Dahlia.

Thankfully, before they stepped inside, the music ended and someone said, "That's it for now, folks. Bluegreen Grass will be back at nine p.m. for their evening performance. CDs are available from your server or the front counter."

Inside, only a handful of people waited, and Kyler stepped over to the counter to give his name. He found Dahlia sitting on the end of a split log bench, those long legs teasing him mightily. He sat next to her and said, "Ten minutes."

"That's nothing." She smiled at him. "I go to church sometimes." She carefully placed her hand in his as if testing the waters. He watched as their fingers joined together, a sensation shooting up his arm and buzzing along his shoulders.

"I'm usually pretty tired on Sundays, as it's the only day I don't go in. Though, sometimes I do, like last week. I usually go to my parents' and have lunch with them."

"I go every week," he said. "Do you think that will be a problem for us?"

"I don't see why," she said, meeting his gaze. He couldn't quite see the depth of her emotions in the dimmer light, so he simply squeezed her hand.

"I'd like to come with you," she said. "I've always liked going to church."

"Why's that?" he asked.

She took a few moments to answer, and Kyler wondered if she would. Finally, she said, "I like being reminded of the good in the world. Sometimes I feel so steeped in the bad, you know?"

Kyler didn't quite know, but he could imagine some of the things she'd seen and been exposed to because of her job. "Why'd you choose to be a police officer?" he asked.

"My father was a police officer," she said, her whole face lighting up. "He'd take me to work with him sometimes, and I couldn't imagine anything better." Her smile made Kyler's whole night and he shifted a tiny bit closer to her.

"He worked his way up to Chief of Police in Vernal," Dahlia said. "It was in my blood to be an officer."

"What's the difference between an officer and a detective?" he asked.

"Well, I don't write tickets. I don't patrol. I don't work for a police department," she said. "I work for a unified police force in this part of the state, and we fall under the state troopers."

"Like McDermott."

"Right, but he's not over me either. Me and Gray, we're…sort of on our own. We handle federal cases that come our way in this part of Utah. We handle some higher-level state things too, like what McDermott does, but he does a lot more patrolling, traffic control, all that kind of stuff." She took a big breath. "Here's a good way to think of it. McDermott finds the bad guys, the pieces to a crime puzzle, and we figure out how all the pieces fit together. We interview, handle witnesses, and put everything together to *solve* the crime."

Kyler liked the way she came alive when she spoke about her work. "Which do you like better? The patrolling or the solving?"

"Definitely the solving."

Smart, strong, and sexy. It was a dangerous combination—one Kyler had no defense against, but he didn't need one.

"So maybe...." Dahlia looked up through her lashes at him. "Maybe—"

"Kyler?" The hostess stood several feet away, two menus in her hand.

He stood with Dahlia and they followed the woman through the restaurant to a table in the corner. "This place is so cool," he said. "I can't believe I've driven past this barn for years and never known what was inside."

The waitress set their menus down and walked away, leaving Kyler to admire the old wooden beams in the ceiling, the eclectic décor on the walls, and the raised stage at the other end of the room.

There was everything from beautiful watercolor paintings of horses and the red bluffs just south of here, to black and white photographs of cowboys, several old horseshoes, and a few cattle skulls nailed to the walls.

He looked back at Dahlia with a smile. "I'm glad we came here."

"Me too." She picked up her menu and looked at it, her dark hair barely falling softly over her shoulders.

"Hey," he said. "You got your hair cut."

She grinned at him then, such a full-watt smile that he realized he hadn't truly seen her smile yet.

"I did. This afternoon." She tossed her hair back and it settled behind her so he could see her bare shoulders.

He swallowed and said, "I like it."

"Thanks."

Kyler picked up his own menu. "What were you saying we could maybe do?"

She didn't look away from the menu. "Well, church is at ten-thirty, right? What if we went together, and then you came with me to lunch with my parents?"

Kyler abandoned the search for the best sandwich on the menu. He'd have to ask the waiter, because his brain had just shorted out. "You want me to meet your parents? Tomorrow?"

"Might as well get it over with." She shrugged and reached for her water glass as the waiter appeared and set it down.

There was something behind those words, but Kyler wasn't the detective and couldn't quite piece together what. He ordered his soda and an appetizer of cheese and bacon fries before asking the teen who'd come to wait on them which was the best sandwich on the menu.

"Do you like steak?"

"Who doesn't like steak?"

The teen grinned and pointed to something called

The Viking. "You'll want that. It's steak, tomato, avocado, some of our special sauce, with a fried egg."

Kyler started salivating just thinking about it. "Yep, that's what I want."

"I can add grilled onions too, if you want." He held his pen at the ready.

Kyler glanced at Dahlia, who was watching him with a sparkle in her eye he didn't quite get. He thought about kissing her later with onion breath and said, "No, I'll pass on the onions."

"And for you?" The waiter twisted toward Dahlia.

"I want the same as him." She nodded toward Kyler and said, "But *with* the onions," as if she knew his reasoning for declining them.

Kyler shook his head and managed to wait until the teenager had moved away before laughing.

"HEY, DAD." Kyler entered his parents' house on Wednesday night to find his father sitting in the front living room, where they usually only entertained guests. "What are you doing in here?"

"Oh, your mother is in a rant about the grill and I figured this would be the best place to wait until she calls for me." He set aside his newspaper, where Kyler knew he was working on the crossword puzzle.

"How's the dating scene?" His dad knew Kyler had been trying to find a girlfriend. Everyone in the family knew. He'd been set up by Jazzy and Fabi more times than he could count. Even Tate had gotten him a date or two through the ranch wives at the horse farm up the canyon where he boarded his horse.

Kyler sat down on the piano bench where his mother had tortured them all with lessons until they could play decently well. "I think I found myself someone." He couldn't help the giddy grin that pulled at his mouth.

His father smiled too. "Oh yeah? Who's the lucky woman?"

"Dahlia Reid?" he said, testing to see if his dad knew her. When nothing registered in his father's blazing blue eyes, Kyler added, "She used to be a police officer here in town. Now she's a detective for the county. Or state. Or something. I don't really get it." He laughed, cutting the sound off when he heard his mother yell from the other room.

"I got it," he told his dad, leaning down to give him a quick half-hug before heading down the hall and into the kitchen. The house where he'd grown up was massively huge, with a table big enough to seat them all inside. His mom had started adding more chairs too, as their family had expanded with spouses and grandchildren. Their weekly dinner fell on Wednesday nights, and Kyler had watched his brothers and sisters come and go for years. He loved the family dinner and hadn't missed it in years, except when he was super sick or way behind on his jobs.

He spotted his mother through the window, standing in the outdoor kitchen with her hands on her hips. She had hair the color of ripe wheat that he knew she maintained with a trip to the salon every month. Her bright blue eyes turned from annoyed to pleased when he stepped outside and said, "What do you need help with, Mom?"

"Kyler, dear, how are you?"

"Just fine." He looked at the grill. "What's goin' on here?" She'd taken out the pieces where the food usually cooked and had laid them haphazardly on the end of the grill where the utensils usually were.

"It won't light."

No wonder his father had retreated to the sitting room to do a crossword puzzle. Kyler moved closer to the grill. "Is there gas in the tank?"

"Of course there is. I know how to check that."

Kyler almost flinched away from her irritated tone, but he checked anyway. The meter on the propane tank was clear. "Mom, this is empty."

"No, I checked it."

He hefted the tank out from the back of the grill. "Look, it's clear. That means no gas."

"No, clear means it's full."

He cocked his head at her, amused by her confusion and slightly annoyed that she didn't believe him. "When's the last time you bought a new propane tank?"

"I don't buy them. Your dad does."

"And what did he say about this?"

She wiped her newly cut bangs out of her face, clearly frustrated. A hint of redness entered her face that had nothing to do with the summer heat. "He said we probably needed a new tank," she mumbled.

A burst of laughter came out of Kyler's mouth. He silenced it quickly at her cross look. "I'll go get a refill," he said. "You put this mess back together."

"Hurry up," she called after him. "Wren and Tate are coming tonight and they're bringing their baby."

Kyler didn't quite understand why that mattered. Dinner wouldn't be ready any faster just because a baby was coming. But whatever. He drove to the hardware store and traded in the empty tank for a new one and got on back to his parents' house as quickly as he could.

He'd just finished hooking up the new tank to the grill when his sister burst through the French doors from the house. "You're dating Dahlia Reid?"

"Hey, Wren," he said. She bounced the cutest little girl on her hip. Etta had been born completely bald and it had taken six months for the baby to grow any hair. It wisped about her face now as she stared at Kyler with a grumpy look on her face.

He walked closer and cooed at her. "Hey, sweet Etta. How are you?"

She smiled and warmed right up to him, and Wren passed the baby to Kyler to hold. "So? Dahlia?"

"Yeah," he said. "We're going out."

"How long has this been going on?"

"Oh, I don't know, Wren." He sighed, the thought of explaining how he and Dahlia had met to the various members of his family one by one overwhelming. "Since I went to the cabin. She was caught out in the—"

Jazzy, one of the twins, burst through the backdoor. "Wait! Are you talking about Dahlia?"

"How do you guys even know about us?" he asked.

"It's a small town," Jazzy said, panting as she caught her breath. Fabi joined them on the patio, her eyes just as wide.

"Dahlia Reid?" Fabi said it like Dahlia wasn't worth his time.

"I talked to a customer in Maple Mountain, who said he saw you with someone at Teddy's," Wren said. "He said she was the detective, and well, that's Dahlia." She gave him a quick smile. "Unless you're dating Gray Salisbury."

"Ha ha," Kyler said. "What's wrong with Dahlia?" he asked Fabi.

"Nothing," she said, a conceited air in her word.

"She's...." Jazzy exchanged a glance with Fabi before continuing with, "Perfect for you, actually."

Kyler rolled his eyes. "Glad my sisters approve."

Tate appeared in the doorway, a huge brown pastry box in his hand that could only mean one thing: doughnuts. He grinned at Kyler. "You and Dahlia. Nice." He maneuvered over to the counter and set the box down. "She's smart. Tough, but I liked her."

Kyler thought Dahlia was actually quite feminine, especially in shorts that only went halfway down her thigh. But he kept that thought to himself as he answered his sister's questions about how they met, when they'd started going out, and if they'd kissed yet.

"Not telling," Kyler said to that question.

"Then you have!" Wren cried triumphantly.

"Come on," he said, tired of the game. He handed the now-sleeping Etta to her dad. "I'm thirty-five-years-old."

"And you owe me ten bucks," Wren said to Fabi, too much glee in her voice.

Fabi glared at Kyler like it was his fault she'd bet on his love life. "I can't believe you've kissed her already. It's only been a couple of weeks."

"And she's been really busy with a big case," Tate added, totally not helping Kyler out at all.

"Bro," he said in warning, and Tate flashed a quick smile before looking down at his sleeping daughter.

"Maybe if you guys had your own boyfriends, you wouldn't be so worried about what I'm doing with Dahlia." Kyler stepped past them as his mother waved at him to come in and get the hamburgers so they could get cooking.

No way he was telling them he'd kissed her within twelve hours of meeting her, but he grinned just thinking about it.

CHAPTER 12

Dahlia threw her pen on top of the folder she'd just closed. "Something's got to break," she said, her voice full of frustration and scorn. "I can't keep going over these files." She stood, grabbing her water bottle. "I'm going for a walk."

"It's a hundred degrees out there," Gray said, sounding bored. "Take more than that tepid water in your bottle."

She ignored him and went straight outside. How he could review the same notes day in and day out, she didn't know. He'd been a detective longer than her; maybe she'd develop the patience required.

But this case...this case was slowly driving her insane. At least the late nights had calmed down a bit. They'd gotten nothing from the sighting at the cabin, other than a more detailed description of the suspect. Jose Garces was a fake name that had led them nowhere. They needed another witness to interview, one with real information.

They had nothing.

Dahlia's long strides took her away from the offices in downtown Beaverton and into the park where she could find relief from the near-July sun in the form of shade. She'd gone out with Kyler again last night, this time right in Brush Creek. He'd told her that his whole family now knew about them, and he'd invited her to the family dinner the following Wednesday.

She still hadn't said a word to her parents about Kyler, and he was going to be eating lunch with them in just forty-eight hours.

She sighed as she found a bench and sat. Dahlia had always been able to release her cares and frustrations to the world once she got outside. It was why she'd grown up hiking in the hills surrounding Vernal, and why she liked a good hard run in the morning. Not lately, as she'd worked so much she could barely peel herself out of bed once the sun rose. But especially in the fall and spring, when the weather was calm and crisp during the dawn.

With her phone on silent and no one else in the park, her restless thoughts and never-ending frustrations started to seep away. She breathed in and then focused on pushing her breath out, relaxing her muscles as she did.

After several minutes, a calm peace descended upon her. She stood and made her way around the park, just a bit of exercise to get her heart beating a tiny bit faster than it did when she sat at her desk.

Sometimes the pieces she'd been playing with on a case would come together on an anti-frustration walks such as this one. With her mind free and able to wander, Dahlia had impressed Gray and their boss with her ability to return to the office with a new idea, something else to research, or a theory which steered them in the right direction.

Today, she couldn't stop thinking about the coyote showing up at Kyler's house in broad daylight. He'd never done anything like that before, choosing to work under the cover of darkness or from inside an unknown location.

Why Kyler's cabin?

Why Sunday morning?

Who had he called? For what? Why had he told Kyler his name at all?

None of it made sense, and the loose, ill-fitting pieces had been tormenting her for almost two weeks.

"Maybe it's his real name," she muttered to herself. "Maybe it's a parent's name. A brother. An uncle. An ancestor."

Around the park she went again, though she was sweating and completely out of water. Why Kyler's cabin?

They'd found nothing at the bluffs to indicate anyone had stayed the night there on that particular weekend. So the coyote had lied about that. She and Gray had been in the area to follow a lead that had never panned out. A man supposedly lived up near Kyler's cabin, completely off the grid, and he'd been spreading stories around Beaverton about people passing his campsite in the night.

Naturally, Dahlia and Gray wanted to find this man and question him. So they'd gone up the canyon two weeks ago to find him and gotten caught in the storm. Since then, no one had seen or heard from him. He'd basically disappeared as quickly as the coyote had.

"Maybe the witness is the coyote," she mused. "Maybe they live off the grid together." Maybe, maybe, maybe.

Because Gray had been correct about the heat and that she needed more water, she returned to the office and filled her water bottle from the ice-cold drinking fountain.

"Hey," she said, lifting her bottle to drink again. "What about going back up there to find that off-grid guy?"

Gray looked up, his eyes guarded and yet hopeful at the same time. "The off-grid guy?"

"The one we were looking for when the storm hit. Who is he? Maybe he *is* the coyote. Maybe our guy didn't go down to the road and hitch a ride somewhere. Maybe he's still up that canyon right now. Maybe he's been coming down to town, spreading rumors about someone else in the hopes that we'll focus on finding anyone but him."

Dahlia was aware that she was speaking too fast, but she couldn't slow herself down.

"That's a lot of what ifs," Gray said.

"Our whole job is what ifs." Dahlia took another long drink from her water bottle. "It's worth following up on. What else have we got?"

Gray glanced at the files he'd been reading for the twentieth time. "Where's the file on that off-grid guy's statement?"

Dahlia grinned and started shuffling paperwork to find the statement they needed. "Right here."

"Let's go over it again."

———

DAHLIA TWISTED to see herself from the back, just to make sure her skirt wasn't too short. The flirty, flowy black fabric swished with the movement, and she decided that if she didn't wear heels, the skirt would be fine.

She owned exactly one pair of heels, and she usually wore them to church. But with this skirt, and the pale pink blouse that almost fell off her shoulder, and she thought a sensible pair of flats would be better.

She smiled at her reflection. "You should go to church more often," she told herself. Dahlia spent a lot of time in her masculine uniform and boring shoes, and she found she liked dressing up from time to time—especially when she was about to meet her boyfriend.

When she opened the door to Kyler's grinning face, she liked the way he drank her in, the heat that entered his eyes, the way he leaned in close and inhaled the scent of her before touching her.

"You ready?" he asked.

"Lead on."

The mood between them was fun, light, playful, as he drove the few minutes from her house to the church right on Main Street. She usually went to the one that sat at the mouth of the canyon, but she didn't mind going anywhere with Kyler. He held her hand on the way in, and though Dahlia caught people looking their way, she didn't mind. She was used to people staring at her.

He led her right down the aisle to a bench filled with people already—his family. Nerves made her lick her lips and clear her throat. All the Fuller eyes turned her way, and Kyler put himself between her and them, quick smiles for everyone.

The pastor got up right after she'd smoothed her skirt down and sat, and she realized Kyler had timed their arrival to the second so there could be no introductions. She'd already confirmed that they needed to leave fifteen minutes before church ended, so she really wouldn't be meeting them until Wednesday.

Kyler took her hand in his and held it on his leg, his attention toward the front of the room. Dahlia copied him, but inside she worried about what her parents would think of him. Particularly her mother.

The pastor seemed to have a kind soul, and he spoke with passion about relying on the Lord for guidance.

Dahlia, admittedly, hadn't done that a whole lot, but as he spoke, she wanted to do a better job of it.

When Kyler nudged her and nodded to the end of the row, Dahlia realized it was time to go. She stood abruptly, glad she hadn't worn the heels so they wouldn't click on the hard wood floor as they made their way out.

"So what did you think?" he asked as they exited the building and stepped into the summer sun.

"I liked him a lot," Dahlia said. "He said good things."

"He usually does." Kyler held her door for her while she got in the truck and made sure she covered her legs with the skirt. With him seated beside her, he exhaled. "So your parents."

"We have to stop at Sweets first. I want to get a chocolate cake."

"Sounds amazing." He eased the truck onto Main Street and on out of town. Dahlia turned up the radio, which Kyler kept on the country music station, and he started to sing along. He had a wonderful, rich, tenor voice, and Dahlia closed her eyes and let her thoughts drift away.

She often worked out problems in this dream-like state as well, but before she knew it, Kyler said, "Sweetheart, do you still want to get a cake?"

Dahlia snapped her eyes open, her pulse spiking as she tried to figure out where they were. "Did I sleep the whole way here?" She yawned, not quite sure when she'd slept so soundly.

"Yep."

"I'm sorry." She glanced at him, a sheepish smile on her face.

"It's fine." He indicated the pastry shop. "We want cake, yes?"

"Yes." She followed him out of the truck. "This was my favorite place growing up," she said. "My father and I used to ride our bikes here and get treats." She stepped through the door as Kyler held it open for her.

"He always paid in cash so my mother wouldn't know." She giggled and drew in a deep breath of the heavenly aroma inside the bakery. "Ah." She smiled at Kyler. "Smell that chocolate?" She practically danced up to the counter.

Kyler chuckled and followed her. "Can we get more than cake?"

Dahlia cuddled into him. "You can get whatever you want."

He ordered a macadamia coconut cookie with lime frosting and a oatmeal chocolate chip cookie. "And the chocolate cake," Dahlia said, pulling out her wallet.

"I got this," Kyler said. He paid and they headed across town to her parents' house. As they pulled up outside the squatty, white brick house, nerves struck Dahlia full in the chest.

"So we talked about this, right?" she asked, swiveling toward Kyler.

"It will be fine," he said.

Dahlia wanted to believe him. Wanted it more than

anything. He got out and she followed him, putting her hand on his arm to stop him. "Hey."

He turned back to her and looked her right in the eye. She let her hand drop, and he made no move to touch her, somehow sensing the weight of the moment.

"I really like you," she said.

Happiness bloomed on his face, and he leaned in close and whispered right in her ear, "I really like you too, Dahlia."

CHAPTER 13

Kyler let Dahlia enter her parents' house first, her words still ringing in his ears. *I really like you.*

Sure, they'd only really known each other for a couple of weeks. But she wasn't new to the dating scene, and neither was he. He knew what he liked, and she obviously did too. He'd shared things with her he'd only told his brothers. She confided in him. And every moment with her felt filled with magic and the hope of many more experiences together.

"Mom?" she called. "They're usually sitting right here." She pointed to the two recliners facing the television in the tiny front room. This whole house could fit inside his parent's kitchen and dining room. But it was clean, with white painted walls and carpet that seemed new in the last five years.

A dining table sat in the far corner, with the kitchen

opposite of that. He glanced down a hall and saw three more doors—bedrooms and a bathroom, he assumed—before following Dahlia outside.

No signs of life existed in the backyard. The Reids live in a quiet neighborhood, and he couldn't even hear a dog barking.

"If they went downstairs...." Anger flashed in Dahlia's eyes as she spun back toward the house. Back inside, a gray cat leapt onto the table, and Kyler watched it as he passed. Not really a fan of cats, he'd learned to give them a wide berth after he'd been scratched from elbow to wrist.

Dahlia opened the first door in the hallway, which led to a set of steps leading down. "Mom? Dad?"

Someone called from down there, and Dahlia practically spat fire. "Leave the cake," she said. "Let's go see if they're okay."

"They can't go downstairs?" he asked.

"No," she said. "They're not supposed to."

"Why not?" He followed her as she practically stomped down the steps.

"Because someone will get hurt," she said, reaching the bottom and pivoting away from him. Kyler had no choice but to go with her, and just as he turned, a man appeared in a doorway leading to a cold storage room.

"Oh, hello there. You must be Kyler."

Caught off guard, Kyler stumbled over his words a little, finally saying, "Uh, yes, yes, sir, I am." He wasn't sure what Dahlia had told them. She'd spent the time warning him about her parents. *Dad is nice. Mom can be standoffish.*

"And you must be Theo, Dahlia's father. I've heard a lot about you."

"Oh really?"

"Yeah." Kyler chuckled, keeping one eye on Dahlia as she reached her mother and said something sharp to her. "Something about a bike ride and Sweets. Oh, and cash."

Her father tilted his head back and laughed, which drew Dahlia's and her mother's attention. She came back toward them. "Dad, you're not supposed to be down here."

"The railing's fine, dear." He gave her a quick peck on the cheek. "We're fine."

Dahlia made a face like she smelled something rotten. "What are you doing down here anyway? We moved everything upstairs."

Kyler glanced around. Sure enough, there was no furniture down here, just one long, empty room with two doors at the end of it.

"We wanted to make Dutch oven peach cobbler." He held up a jar of peaches.

"I told you we'd bring dessert," Dahlia said. "There isn't even a fire going, Dad. There's not time for peach cobbler." She spoke with exasperation in her voice, and Kyler wanted to diffuse the situation for her.

Her mother shuffled over and cleared her throat. "Hello. I'm Darby Reid." She pinned Dahlia with a look that meant business. What that business was,

Kyler wasn't sure. He only knew he didn't want to find out.

"Of course," Kyler said. "I'm Kyler Fuller."

"And you're dating my daughter." She definitely didn't approve of that.

Dahlia had hinted that her mother wouldn't approve, so Kyler hitched a smile on his face and said, "Yep."

Somehow that single syllable word was wrong, because Darby Reid frowned.

"Mom, not now." Dahlia put her hand through her father's elbow and handed the peaches to Kyler. "I'll help you up."

"I really am fine," her dad said, but with his first step Kyler saw the limp, the weakness in his left leg, and he suddenly understood why Dahlia didn't want him going up and down the steps.

It took an agonizingly long time for him to climb the steps, and when Kyler reached the top, he watched as Theo collapsed into the recliner, panting and sweating. Dahlia turned, her face flaming red, and helped her mother up the last few stairs.

Foolishness pulsed through Kyler. He hadn't even thought to help her mother up. He'd been so focused on her father's obvious injury, he hadn't thought that her mother would require assistance too.

With her mom seated in the other recliner, Dahlia said, "So what's for dinner?"

"I was going to do steak and potatoes," her father wheezed.

"But you hadn't built a fire yet." Dahlia took a few steps and entered the kitchen. Unsure of where he belonged, Kyler went with her. She pulled ingredients out and set a pot of water on the stove.

"Will you do the steaks, please?" she whispered. "I'll make mashed potatoes and see if there's any corn in the garden." She stepped away before he could answer that of course he'd take care of the steaks.

Before he knew it, she'd slid open the glass door and left him in the house with her parents. "So Dahlia tells me you were the Chief of Police," he said to her dad. "What about you, Darby? What did you do?"

"Do?" The woman's shrill voice could've called dogs. "I raised Dahlia, of course. Rearing children is a full-time job, you know. Dahlia's got herself all mixed up in that police work." She *tsk*ed like Dahlia's job was terrible. "She'll never be able to be a mother and a detective."

"Darby," Theo said, a clear warning in his voice. Kyler laid out the steaks and started opening cupboards to find the salt and pepper.

"It's probably fine." She patted her hair, which looked like it had been set recently. "She can't find a decent man anyway."

Kyler's fingers froze though he'd just located the spices.

"That's her boyfriend right there," Theo hissed. "Stop it."

He swept the salt and pepper down from their perch and seasoned the steaks. "I'll be right back." He passed Dahlia coming in with an armful of corn as he went out to start the grill. Thankfully, it lit with the press of a button so he didn't have to find matches or a lighter. He could've gone back inside, made polite conversation, but he didn't.

She can't find a decent man anyway.

He hoped he was decent enough for her—and her mother.

When the grill was hot enough, he put the steaks on and checked the time on his phone. His father had taught him to cook steak to a perfect medium by using time and temperature. He'd second-guessed himself his first few times, but he'd learned that four minutes on the first side, and four on the second would give him the results he wanted.

Eight more minutes until he had to go back inside and face her parents again. He finally returned to the house with perfectly cooked meat to find the tension had tripled since he'd left. Everyone sat in complete silence, and all three of them looked miserable.

"Steaks are ready," he announced. "Dahlia, what do you need help with?"

"Setting the table," she said. "Please."

"Point me in the right direction for utensils and plates."

She wouldn't look at him, but opened a cupboard

and a drawer, and he got to work. "What do you do now to keep busy, Theo?" he asked.

"Not much."

So there would be no help in the conversation. Kyler fell silent and finished with the cups just as Dahlia pulled the corn from the boiling water. "We're ready," she announced.

Her parents got up and joined them at the dining room table. Her father said grace, and food got passed around, but Kyler didn't feel anywhere close to how he felt at his family dinners.

This was horrible, suffocating silence that cut off his airway and made swallowing almost impossible. No one complimented him on the steaks. No one said anything.

"We have to go," Dahlia said as soon as she'd finished eating.

"But we haven't had cake," Kyler said, wondering what had flipped her from his wonderful, giggly Dahlia in the bakery to this nervous, red-faced woman who couldn't look anyone in the eye.

"You guys keep it," she said, gathering her phone. "Gray texted, and I need to go." She marched toward the front door, leaving him with her parents once more.

"I'm sorry," he said. "I don't know—"

"We're fine," her father said, solidifying that the man was an eternal optimist, probably used to tense meals like this between his wife and daughter.

Her mother didn't look at him at all, even when he said, "Thank you for having us, Darby."

So he hadn't passed the test. At least he could breathe once he'd left the house behind. Dahlia sat on her side of the truck, pressed right up against the passenger door like he'd contracted a contagious disease and she didn't want to get it.

"Wow," he said as he sat down and twisted the key. "That was intense. I mean, you said it would be, but—"

"I don't want to talk about it." Dahlia put her elbow on the window ledge and leaned her head into her hand, completely closed off from him.

Kyler didn't know what to do. In his family, they talked about their issues with each other. Came face-to-face and worked things out. Dahlia's family was apparently much different in that regard.

He let a few minutes of silence go by as they put Vernal in their rear-view mirror. "What's wrong?" he asked.

"Nothing."

"Dahlia." He glanced at her, but she was immovable.

Miles went by, and Kyler's mind churned. "Was it just because they went in the basement?"

"Just because?" she repeated, finally whipping her face toward him. "My father could fall and break his hip. He'd be dead before my mom could do anything about it. Neither of them seem to get that."

"What happened to his leg?" he asked.

"He got injured on the job." She turned back to the window, that conversation clearly closed.

Kyler didn't know what else to say, especially because

Dahlia didn't seem like she'd hear anything he said anyway. But as he pulled into her driveway, he had to try one more time. "What did they say to you while I was outside?"

Because something had been said. She hadn't been the color of boiled lobster when he'd gone outside. Her eyes hadn't been slightly puffy. And he'd never seen someone eat so fast.

"Gray didn't text, did he?"

Dahlia finally turned from her vigil out the passenger window. "Kyler...I don't think we should see each other anymore."

A load of bricks dropped onto his lungs, forcing all the air out. "What?" he gasped. "Why not?"

A single tear fell from her gorgeous eyes and trailed down her cheek. "I just don't think we're a match." She twisted back to the door and opened it, practically falling out of the truck. "I'm sorry I wasted your time," she said before slamming the door shut and striding away with a surety he couldn't argue with.

CHAPTER 14

Dahlia collapsed against the front door once she'd closed and locked it, her sobs coming quickly now. She'd held them in for the long drive back from Vernal, and just barely.

You think he'll be satisfied being Mr. Mom?

You're delusional, Dahlia. You can't be a detective and a wife. It's not possible.

Even when her father had tried to come to her rescue, her mother had silenced him with cruel words. *You were never here, Theo. Never. You think that was a good life for me? For Dahlia?*

And her mother's eyes, so sharp and so penetrating, had cut them both into silence, the way she often did.

He seems nice, Dahlia, but he's a doormat. If you think for one moment he can keep working and the two of you can raise a family, you're wrong.

Wrong.

Wrong.

Wrong.

Her mom had always disapproved of Dahlia's job, but these remarks had gone deeper than previous jabs. Dahlia honestly hadn't given much thought to a family, because she'd never found the right man. As she thought about Kyler's shocked eyes, his utter disbelief at her statement that they shouldn't see each other anymore, she wondered if he could've fallen for her as fast as she'd fallen for him. Perhaps she'd made the biggest mistake of her life.

She stood and whipped open the door, sure Kyler would still be sitting in his truck. Maybe he'd even be standing on her doorstep, waiting for her to come to her senses and talk to him.

He was gone.

She stepped back and let the door swing closed. Her phone started chiming, one after the other, indicating five new messages. She half-hoped it would be Gray, telling her about a huge break in their case. If she could just get the coyote out of her life, maybe she'd have room for other things.

I don't know what happened when I was outside, Kyler's first message said.

It doesn't really matter to me.

I really like you, and I think we're a fine match.

I get you have a lot going on right now.

I can wait.

Dahlia stared at the last three words, hope taking root in her heart. At the same time, was it fair of her to put him on hold every time she had a difficult case? Every time something came along that she deemed more important than him, would he wait then?

Her hope withered as quickly as it had started to bloom. She'd heard some of Gray's stories about his family falling apart. The job came first for him, and it always had for Dahlia too. She'd never had much to put before it—until Kyler.

Ally mewed, and Dahlia scooped the cat into her arms, tears coming again. "I'm being ridiculous, right?" she asked the animal. "I mean, we've been seeing each other for two weeks. It's not like we're in love or he's asked me to marry him."

The cat squirmed in her arms, and Dahlia put her down before she got scratched. She set some coffee to brew and wondered what to do with herself for the rest of the afternoon. She'd planned to spend it with Kyler, falling madly in love—because she *had* started down that path, and she knew it.

She wished she had some cake to go with her coffee, but the bakery in town was closed on Sunday. So she pulled down a recipe book and got to work making one of her own. Every time her phone chimed, she jumped. And she couldn't just ignore it, as the message might be from Gray.

But then the fact that she worried more about a text

from Gray than from Kyler gnawed at her, making her stomach writhe and frustration boil inside her. With the cake finally in the oven, Dahlia sat down with her phone.

It's unfair of me to make you wait, she texted to Kyler. *There will always be another case keeping us apart.*

She stared at the words, horrified at the truth in them. Did it really come down to that impossible choice? Her job or an opportunity to live her life?

Glancing around her house, she knew she didn't really live. She never took time for herself the way Kyler did when he went to the cabin. She didn't have any hobbies outside of work. She ran to stay in shape. She hiked to know the terrain she was responsible for knowing. She visited her parents out of obligation.

A sense of sadness draped over her as she realized the only bright speck in her life in the last several years had been Kyler. And she'd just removed him from the equation.

He didn't respond, and she wondered where he'd gone. Was he sitting home too, miserable, with a chocolate cake in the oven he'd eat all by himself?

She texted Gray next. *I need advice. Can I call you?*

Advice? He always responded within seconds. *Work stuff or personal stuff?*

Personal. It's about Kyler Fuller.

Her phone rang ten seconds later, and she swiped on the call from Gray.

"I'm not much good at this stuff," he said by way of hello. "But I can try."

Dahlia didn't know what to say now that she had him on the phone. "Does the job always have to come first?"

A lengthy pause told her Gray was really trying to find the right answer. "I think that varies from person to person," he said. "For me, I chose that. Was I right?" He exhaled, and his voice was heavier and more morose when he said, "I honestly don't know. I lost my wife and my daughter. I love the job, but is it worth that? I guess at some point, I thought it was."

Dahlia inhaled the scent of baking chocolate and tried to organize her thoughts.

"You're serious with Kyler Fuller already?" Gray asked. "It's been, what? Sixteen days?"

The fact that he knew that testified of what a great detective Gray Salisbury was.

"Sometimes you just hit it off," she said. "How long did you know Julie before you knew?"

"Oh, I knew we'd get married after the first date. She took some convincing." He chuckled, the sound petering out pretty quickly. "You went and visited your parents today, didn't you?"

"Kyler came to meet them."

"Dahlia," Gray said with a sharp dose of reproving in his voice. "You're letting her do it again."

Dahlia wanted to play dumb. Ask something like, "Who?" or "Do what?" but she knew. She'd told Gray about her previous boyfriends and how her mother had always run them off.

"Why do you think she does it?" she asked. "We're detectives. What's my mother's motivation for keeping me single?"

"I don't know." Gray sighed. "Maybe she doesn't want to lose you. Maybe she thinks you'll stop coming to visit on Sundays if you've got someone else in your life."

Leaning back against the couch, Dahlia let her eyes drift closed, her feelings circling, chasing after her thoughts. "I don't think that's it."

She heard her mother's words in her mind again. You were never here, Theo. Never. You think that was a good life for me? For Dahlia?

"I think she doesn't want me to be with someone, because she knows what it's like to have a spouse that's married to their job. She doesn't want someone else to have to go through that." As she spoke, Dahlia felt the truth in her speculation. "I never realized my mother was unhappy," she added, her voice barely a whisper.

"I didn't know Julie was either," Gray said, just as somber. "Until the day I got home in the middle of the night to find she'd taken Carla and left."

Dahlia hadn't heard this story, and she said, "I'm so sorry, Gray. Kyler told me about his previous girlfriend and how she left town in the middle of the night too. He said it was devastating, and he looked so sad...." She imagined the anguish on her partner's face, matching it with that she'd seen in Kyler's eyes.

He'd asked her to communicate with him. Let him know she was safe and that she'd be coming home at night. She knew that he couldn't handle another ghosting, and she wondered if she'd just done that. Broken up with him with little to no explanation.

"Dahlia," Gray said. "Maybe for you, this job doesn't have to come first."

Dahlia wanted to protest, say she'd worked her whole career to have this job, that she couldn't give it up. But the words wouldn't come. "I'll think about it," she said. "I have to go. The timer on my cake is going off."

"All right. Text me later."

Dahlia hung up and stared at the blank television in front of her. So she'd lied. The cake still had twenty more minutes in the oven. She wanted to *stop* thinking about what she should do about Kyler, but he absolutely wouldn't leave her mind.

———

He didn't text until the next morning, five words that left her reeling.

Only if you let it.

She'd said there would always be another case keeping them apart, and that was what he'd said.

Dahlia didn't know what to do. When she wrote the wrong thing in her report for the third time, she growled and got up from her desk.

"Kyler?" Gray called after her, but Dahlia ignored him, gripping her phone too tight, too tight, as she went outside.

She dialed Kyler and put the phone to her ear, already at an utter loss as to what to say to him.

"Dahlia," he answered, his voice a balm to her anger, calming her weary soul and her frenzied mind.

"I don't want to let it," she blurted. "But it's my job, and I don't know how to be anything but who I am."

After several beats of silence, each one increasing Dahlia's anxiety, he said, "Come to my family dinner on Wednesday, like we planned."

She'd not been expecting him to say that. Or anything remotely close to it. "I—"

"Dinner's at six-thirty. I'll make sure there's chocolate cake." He wasn't leaving her any room to get out of it, and Dahlia didn't want to get out of it.

"We need to iron some things out," she said, a non-committing answer.

"Let's go to dinner tonight."

An ache started in her chest, right where her heart beat. "Kyler…."

"Dahlia, I'm trying here," he said. "I'm choosing you. I want to be with you. I think we're great together, and I haven't felt about anyone in a long time the way I feel about you." He paused, an angry, frustrated sigh coming through the line. "If you don't feel the same, I can accept that. Eventually. But I think you *do* feel the same, and you're just, I don't know what. Scared? Worried about something that hasn't even happened yet? Something."

Tears pricked Dahlia's eyes at the same time Gray stuck his head out the door and gestured to her. "I have to go," she said, her voice much too high. "I'll text you later."

"I'll be at Ruby's at seven," he said. "You're welcome to join me."

She didn't commit either way, but said, "Goodbye," and hung up before hurrying to see what Gray needed.

CHAPTER 15

Kyler waited at Ruby's until eight-thirty. Dahlia didn't show up. He felt like she'd ripped his lungs out and hung them up to dry on a clothesline. He couldn't get a proper breath, and he lay in bed, staring at the ceiling until utter exhaustion forced his eyes closed and his body to rest.

She didn't come to the family dinner on Wednesday either. Thankfully, he hadn't told anyone she would be there, so he didn't have to endure endless questions about why she hadn't made it.

They ran through his mind though. She texted him several times throughout the day, and he responded. Nothing too serious, he realized. She was letting him know she was safe, still working on the case, and that she hoped it would be wrapped up soon.

Kyler pushed the potato salad around his plate,

wondering if it even mattered if this case ended soon. As she'd said, there'd always be another one.

"What's wrong with you?" Berlin, the youngest Fuller child, asked as she sat down next to him. "You usually inhale the potato salad and have seconds before we've all had some."

"Nothing," he muttered, forking a bite of the salad into his mouth. It tasted too acidic today, and he could barely swallow it.

Milt sat down directly across from him, putting his son's plate beside him. The long picnic table had been built to accommodate the whole family, and Kyler usually loved sitting out in the yard, the tall trees above them whispering in the breeze as they ate.

"Oh, boy," Milt said after one glance at Kyler. "Things over with Dahlia already?"

Kyler cut a look at Milt and then Berlin. "Dahlia?" she asked. She hadn't been at the last family dinner, where the rest of his sisters had grilled him mercilessly.

"I don't know," he said.

"You don't know?" Milt took a bite of his hot dog.

Kyler shrugged. "I don't know."

Milt wiped the ketchup from his mouth. "How do you not know if you're dating someone or not?"

"I just don't."

"What did she say?"

"She said we shouldn't see each other anymore, but then she calls me and texts me and...I don't know what we are."

She wouldn't go out with him, hadn't met him here tonight though he'd texted the address and menu and what time they ate hours ago. She hadn't responded to that message at all.

Wren sat down on his other side, her baby balanced carefully on her hip. "What's going on?"

"Nothing," Kyler said, shooting Milt and then Berlin a look.

Like that would stop them. "Dahlia somebody broke up with Kyler," Berlin said.

Kyler growled, but Wren paused and looked at him. "Oh, I'm sorry. I know you really liked her."

"Did he?" Milt asked as if Kyler wasn't right there, in the middle of all these siblings. "How do you know that?"

"The way he talked about her last week." Wren fed a potato chunk to Etta. "It was obvious with what he said and how he glowed."

"I didn't glow," he grumbled.

"Hmm," Milt said. "Maybe he's in love with her."

"I'm not in love with her."

"Seemed like he could probably get there," Wren said, like Kyler hadn't even spoken. "They went to church together on Sunday too. Kept her way down on the end though, like he didn't want to share her with us." She narrowed her eyes and looked at Kyler. "So maybe he is in love with her."

"It's been two weeks," Kyler practically yelled. "I'm not in love with her."

"There is such a thing as love at first sight," Wren said to Milt. "Don't you think?"

"Sure," Milt said, sliding his eyes past Kyler in the most annoying way. "And Kyler's been out with at least a dozen women in the past six months. I think he knows who he likes and who he doesn't."

"I hate you guys," Kyler said, rising to his feet. Berlin and Wren sat so close, he couldn't get out from under the picnic table. "I'm not in love with her." He'd said it three times now, and he doubted himself a little more each time. "I'm going to the cabin."

"No, you can't," Wren said, putting her hand on his forearm. "You've got two big jobs tomorrow, and you're scheduled all weekend too. The Oscars' wedding, remember?"

He glared down at her. "Can I go next weekend then?"

"I'll check and let you know. And I won't schedule anything new if you're free."

"Sit down," Milt said, scooping his potato salad onto Kyler's plate. "We'll stop teasing you."

Kyler sat, only because moping around his house alone was worse than enduring conversations with his family. He was so tired of being alone. Working alone. Eating breakfast and lunch and dinner alone.

Is it too much to ask for a companion? he asked the Lord. *You gave Adam Eve. Why can't I have someone?*

He knew he didn't just want someone.

Dahlia Reid, he thought, closing his eyes and laying

his head in his folded arms. *I want Dahlia Reid, Lord. Is that too much to ask?*

The wind in the trees picked up, and Kyler wasn't sure if that was his answer or not. If it was, he didn't know what God was trying to tell him.

When his sisters left, and only Milt remained at the table, Kyler asked, "How do you know when you're in love?" He looked up at his oldest brother, his best friend since Brennan had left for California. "I mean, I thought I was in love with Katie, and she left me with a note on the front door. Maybe I'm just really bad at this."

Milt's eyes softened. "You just know, Kyler. And you're not bad at this."

"I'm thirty-five-years-old."

"So what? That's not that old or anything."

"I'm tired of being alone."

"I know you are, bud. I know you are." Milt looked genuinely sympathetic. "Get up to the cabin, and you'll know what to do."

———

THE DAYS until Kyler could get to the cabin seemed impossibly long and also incredibly short. He made sure the Oscars had a beautiful yard for the wedding, and he got all the soccer fields done in time for the weekend games.

Dahlia's calls dwindled to zero, and her text frequency fell off too. Kyler wasn't sure if he should push her or let her come to him. What he was sure of was that he couldn't survive another weekend in the same town as her and not be with her. So, on Friday afternoon, he loaded up BB and his bike in the back of his truck and headed to the cabin.

As he crested the hill and the cabin came into view, warring emotions hit him. A sense of relief that he'd arrived at his sanctuary came first, followed by a sharp sensation that something wasn't right at the cabin.

He stopped the truck before the tires crunched over the gravel parking area out front. The cabin looked the same. Square structure, with a big front porch that extended from corner to corner. The white door sat closed, with the two windows flanking the door showing nothing but the curtains.

Maybe it was because the crime scene team had been here for days after Kyler left. Maybe they'd changed the aura of the place, moved little things that caught Kyler's eye, like the hose coming off the front of the porch. That hadn't been there before.

He scanned the small yard, which only had a couple of trees, and saw a shoelace tied to a low branch on the tree closest to the forest on the west side. Where had that come from? Who had put it there?

An image of Jose Garces flashed through his mind, but Kyler dismissed it. That man was long gone, as Gray, Dahlia, and every law enforcement agency in this county had been looking for him for months.

BB yipped, and Kyler startled, his heart suddenly

racing with adrenaline. The little dog could've been wondering why Kyler was just sitting in the truck. But he'd put his front paws up on the dashboard of the truck, his gaze trained on the cabin, and barked again.

"What is it?" Kyler asked, straining to see what the corgi could.

BB barked again and again, and Kyler pulled out his phone just as two people came around the west corner of the cabin. Disbelief tore through him that other people were at his property. Both women, they approached the truck at a steady clip.

He glanced down at his phone as BB went nuts, barking and jumping from the seat to the dashboard and back again and again.

Kyler opened Dahlia's text thread when someone knocked on the driver's side window. Five sharp bangs and Kyler turned to stare straight into the glittering, dangerous eyes of Jose Garces.

The coyote.

CHAPTER 16

Dahlia couldn't bring herself to face Kyler in the flesh. She hated that she couldn't, but she was still working out where she was with him, where she wanted to be, and what all that entailed.

She went to church, but he didn't show up and sit with his family. One of his sisters caught her eye and looked like she might say something, but Dahlia must've put off some serious *please don't* vibes, because the blonde pressed her lips together and continued down the aisle, where she slid onto the Fuller family bench and bent close to one of Kyler's brothers and whispered furiously.

She liked how she felt at church, and when she'd asked God what her course of action should be regarding Kyler, her only answer had been patience.

Patience for what, she didn't know. And was she supposed to have more patience, and a new answer would come? Or was it Kyler who should be exercising his patience with her? As far as Dahlia could tell, he already was.

She and Gray had been all over the mountains and hills, up the canyon, from the top of the bluff to the bottom, and they hadn't turned up anything new about the coyote.

"Maybe this will never be solved," she told him on Thursday afternoon.

He gave her a look that was part disbelief and part annoyance. "We solve all our cases."

"It's been seven months. Almost eight."

"And he's still moving people and drugs right through our county," Gray said. "We'll get him."

Dahlia showed up at work on Friday morning with two coffees and a dozen doughnuts. "Today's the day," she proclaimed to Gray, who accepted the coffee and asked, "Any sugar?"

"I already doctored it up for you," she said. "And I got you one of those double-fried apple croissants you like."

He grinned like a little boy who'd just been told he could skip his nightly bath and reached for the brown pastry box. The scent of maple and chocolate came from it as he lifted the lid and Dahlia decided she could enjoy the maple twist she liked so much. She'd been up since five and had put ten miles on the treadmill.

"Today's the day for what?" Gray asked after

chomping through half the croissant and washing it down with his obscenely sugary coffee.

"I don't know," Dahlia said. "But it has to be something."

Gray watched her as she woke her computer and reached for a new case that had come across her desk the day before. "What did you decide to do about Kyler?"

She gave him a peek out of the corner of her eye. "Today might be the day I decide."

Half a smile tugged at Gray's mouth. "He seemed like a good guy." He finished the croissant. "And what about your parents?"

"I haven't spoken to them."

"You didn't go to lunch on Sunday?" His eyebrows went straight up. "You didn't mention that earlier."

"You didn't ask, and I didn't want to talk about it." She flipped open the folder to find a gruesome picture of cattle inside. "Oh—okay. What's this?" She closed the file and picked up her cinnamon and sugar twist, frosted with maple icing.

"A rancher east of here and north of Vernal has had twenty-one cows killed in the past six weeks," Gray said, pulling his own paperwork toward him. "At first, he thought it was coyotes or wolves, but none of his chickens have been hurt. None of his sheep. Only the cattle, and only on the weekends. He thinks his neighbor might be responsible somehow. We need to go see them both today."

"Let's go." She took her coffee to go, and answered

Gray's questions about her parents on the drive over to the ranch.

"And I just told them I needed a week off and that I'd be back this weekend," she finished.

"And will you go?" he asked.

She sighed and pushed her sunglasses further up her nose. "Yeah, probably. It's not really my mother's fault."

"You're right," Gray said. "It's your father's." He gave her a pointed look, and Dahlia turned to look out the passenger window.

"I don't want to do that to Kyler," she said softly.

"Then don't."

"You think I should quit?" Her reflection glinted back at her in the glass, and she wished she looked happier.

"I think you should follow your heart," Gray said, making the turn from paved road to dirt. "Before it's too late. Take it from someone who knows what 'too late' feels like."

He moved on to something else after that, and Dahlia was grateful for him as a partner. She'd always liked Gray, and he'd been tough with her in just the way she needed when she'd started as his partner. It was nice to be able to talk about real life with him too, because he understood the situation perfectly, when no one else could.

Hours later, after both interviews had been completed, Dahlia drove the cruiser back toward Beaverton. The turn-off for the canyon road, where Kyler's cabin was, approached, and she couldn't help feeling like she should drive up there. The craving to see Kyler, hear his voice, yanked through her, making her fingers tighten on the steering wheel.

After she pulled into the parking lot and Gray had gone back inside, Dahlia stayed in the car. It was almost the weekend. Maybe she and Kyler could go to dinner that night. Spend Saturday and Sunday together, hiking, fishing, anything.

She pulled out her phone to call him, something she'd stopped doing when it became too hard to think of something to tell him besides "I don't know."

Follow your heart.

Before it's too late.

Before she could tap or swipe, a text came in. A text from Kyler.

He

"He?" Dahlia read out loud. "What does that mean?" Her heart thrashed in her chest, and she jumped from the car and practically sprinted into the office. "Gray, I need you."

She waved her phone as she wound through the maze of desks to Gray's, where he'd selected two more doughnuts and was working through them while he wrote reports on the interviews they'd done.

"Look."

He studied the phone. "He?" He glanced up at Dahlia. "What does that mean?"

"I don't know." She worried her bottom lip between her teeth. "And he hasn't sent anything else."

"Maybe it's the beginning of another word," he said.

"Hey," Dahlia said. "He's, heard, heading...." She sifted through her mind, searching for words that Kyler would use to start a text that began with *he*.

"Hello," Gray added.

Their eyes met, and they said in unison, "Help."

Dahlia's pulse bumped in her neck, banged against her breastbone. "That's it."

"Dahlia—"

"Gray, I can *feel* it." She stepped around him to her desk and snatched her purse. "I'm following my heart on this one."

"I'm coming," he said.

"It's not necessary." She strode past him and toward the door.

"Of course it's not. I'm coming anyway." Gray darted in front of her and held the door so she could dash through it. "I'll drive."

"Civilians," she said. "We have to be civilians."

He glanced at her, his boots eating the distance to his sedan quickly. "Why?"

"If he's in trouble...." She shook her head and lifted her phone to her ear, the number she'd been searching for finally found and dialed. "Having two detectives show up won't be helpful."

"He could just be hurt," he said. "Maybe something with a lawn mower—"

Dahlia held up her hand to silence him as a woman answered the call with, "Jack of All Trades, this is Wren. How can I help you?"

"Wren, hi," Dahlia said, her voice definitely slipping into her no-nonsense detective tone. "It's Dahlia Reid. I just got a text from Kyler and I'm worried about him. Where can I find him?"

"What kind of text?"

"Is he out on a job?" Dahlia asked, ignoring his sister's question.

"No," Wren said, the panic evident in just those two letters. "He went up to the cabin this afternoon. He'll be there all weekend."

"The cabin," she said to Gray. "Thank you, Wren. I'll call you soon." She hung up, her nerves wringing themselves into knots. "He's at the cabin," she repeated though Gray had obviously heard her and turned toward the road that would take them there.

"Maybe he was just going to invite you to come up and see him," Gray said.

"Maybe." But they hadn't texted in a few days now. Dahlia couldn't shake the feeling that the *he* was only the first half of *help*. She wouldn't rest until she knew for certain.

Please keep him safe, she prayed.

"We've been up there so much," she said. "What did we miss?"

"We didn't miss anything," Gray said. We've been to every dwelling, walked every inch of the forests."

"Hurry anyway," Dahlia said, her eyes scanning everything as Gray pressed a little harder on the accelerator.

———

THE ROOF of the cabin came into view first and Gray eased up the hill. "Dahlia," he said, his voice set high on danger.

"That's Kyler's truck," she whispered. "Stop here."

Gray pulled over about two hundred yards from the cabin. "He didn't pull all the way onto the gravel," he noted.

"That's odd." Dahlia scanned the surroundings, the cabin, searching searching searching for anything out of the ordinary. "Why didn't he pull all the way up?"

"What's on the ground there by the truck? Driver's side."

Dahlia sucked in a breath. "That's BB, his dog." She met Gray's eye for half a second before both of them went back to maintaining a proper vigil. "Something's definitely wrong. We need to call it in. Get people up here."

Movement in the window to the right of the front door of the cabin had Dahlia ducking. "Down," she hissed and Gray joined her. "Right front window. Movement. Curtain movement."

Gray started tapping the screen of his phone, sending messages.

The urge to check again, see what was going on, almost drove Dahlia to the point of insanity. Gray said, "They're forty minutes out."

Dahlia thought that might as well be forty days and forty nights. How long ago had Kyler's text come in? She checked her own phone and quickly calculated the math. Thirty-nine minutes. They'd really been speeding to get there that fast.

Please let him be okay, she thought. *Give him strength and help him say the right things.*

"All right," Gray said, peeking up. "I don't see anything. How do you want to play this?"

"Lost hikers?"

"In our badges and police boots?"

"I could go in alone," Dahlia said, unleashing her hair from its customary work ponytail. She shook it so the curls could loosen up. She unpinned her badge and set it on the dashboard. "Do you have a backpack?"

"Maybe in the back storage bin." Gray frowned. "I'm not thrilled about you going in alone."

"You look too much like a cop," she said. "I'll be fine." She pulled a tube of lip gloss out of her purse and slicked some on. Then she eased open the door, her eyes on the house the whole time. A long metal storage compartment ran along the truck, right behind the cab. She opened it and hit the jackpot. Not only did a backpack sit there, but a red flannel shirt she quickly tied around her waist, as well as a wadded up gray T-shirt with the Ruby's Roost logo on the chest. She crouched as she unbuttoned her tan detective shirt and slipped the T-shirt over her head. Even though she couldn't do anything about the black police boots, with the backpack in place, she might be able to pass for someone who'd stumbled upon the cabin while wandering the hills.

With one final glance at the cabin, she darted into the trees off the side of the road, running through the foliage until she felt good and sweaty, like she'd been hiking for a while.

Then she faced west, squared her shoulders, and headed back toward the cabin.

CHAPTER 17

Kyler kept working at the restraints the coyote had bound his hands with. It wasn't tape, and it wasn't metal, but somewhere in between. He'd gotten out of the truck willingly, and the man had tied him immediately and passed him to the two women.

BB had barked and barked, and Kyler had thrashed against the women and the restraints when he heard his dog yelp.

"What did you do to my dog?" Kyler asked again as the man paced the room, his thumbnail in his mouth, his sharp eyes on the windows. He was obviously waiting for someone. Or something.

The two women had disappeared down the hall leading the bedrooms, and Kyler could hear intermittent crying coming from that direction. At least he thought it was crying.

The man didn't answer his question. Again. Just

pivoted when he was almost to where Kyler sat in the dining room area and went back toward the fireplace, his head swiveling so he could keep his eyes on the windows and door.

When he was farthest away, one step from turning back, Kyler inched his chair closer to the kitchen cabinets. He wasn't tied to the chair, but he didn't dare make a move toward the first drawer where he knew a pair of scissors was concealed. He wasn't sure how much time he'd have, and he'd rather have a guarantee than a quick hope.

He'd moved probably a foot closer and the coyote hadn't noticed. He just paced and paced. Kyler wasn't sure how much time had gone by, but his patience was wearing thin. He moved again, his shoulder almost touching the counter now. One more pace, and he should be there.

The coyote froze down by the fireplace, and Kyler heard the whistling and footsteps on the front porch a moment later. He eased open the drawer with his elbow, never happier for the easy-glide system he'd spent a couple of days helping his father install the summer after he'd graduated from high school.

"Hello?" A woman's voice came through the wood, and the coyote's eyes narrowed. Knocking sounded, but Kyler wasn't at the right angle to be able to see who stood on the porch. "Anyone here? I'm lost and I just need some help getting back to the trail."

The coyote looked at Kyler, pure malice shining in his dark eyes. "You?"

"I came alone," Kyler said, the word almost like poison on his tongue. The coyote focused on the door again, and Kyler lifted himself off the chair just enough to get his hands into the drawer and around the pair of scissors. He slipped them into his back pocket and sat at the same time the coyote opened the door six inches, his body blocking any view Kyler might have had.

"Oh, hey." The woman laughed, and Kyler's blood ran cold. He knew that laugh. And he knew Dahlia was not lost and didn't need help getting back to the trail. She'd gotten his text and somehow figured out he'd been trying to spell *help me that man is back and I think he's your guy.*

Or something. Kyler wasn't exactly sure what he would've texted her. He just knew she was the first person he'd thought of texting, and the last person he wanted to see every evening.

He'd missed part of the conversation at the door, but the man wasn't budging, not even an inch. He closed the door and gestured for Kyler to stand. "Out," he said in that smooth voice that didn't soothe.

"Out where?" Kyler made his voice as loud as he dared without being obvious.

The man grabbed Kyler by the collar and heaved him to his feet, dragging him around the peninsula in the countertop and thrusting him into the mudroom. "Stay. Silent." He put his finger to his lips in the most sinister way. The door closed, and Kyler scrambled for the scissors to cut himself free.

If Dahlia was here, Gray wouldn't be far. And neither would backup. Kyler needed to get his hands workable, and get the woman he loved away from danger.

I love her, he thought as he maneuvered the blades of the scissors between his wrists. The sense of euphoria was quickly replaced with the intensity of the task at hand. He wasn't sure he could even cut through this material, but he squeezed as hard as he could, and his hands popped free. Keeping the scissors in his hand, he moved as silently as he could out the back door.

He pressed his back against the house, his fingers curling around the corner. "Okay." He blew out his breath and peeked around the side of the house. He couldn't see anything from here.

Crouching, he ran along the length of the cabin to the front corner, a prayer streaming through his mind. *Be at the door. Please be at the door.* He peered up through the slats and saw Dahlia's black police boots there.

"Run," he hissed. "Dahlia, you need to go. Now."

She tilted her head and then turned her chin in his direction. Her eyes met his, and he jerked his head toward the road. "Go. Now."

Surprise registered on her face, then a glimmer of fear, all in under a second. She fell back one step when the door opened again. "You can come in now," the man said in that disturbingly perfect voice.

Dahlia pasted her smile back into place and stepped

into the cabin with, "Thanks so much. I won't bother you for long."

"No," Kyler whispered. But he couldn't go in there again. Armed with only a pair of scissors, he was no match for the coyote. He looked out toward the road and made a dash to his truck. Crouched behind the tailgate, he wondered how quickly he could get to someone with a phone. Without keys and without a way to communicate, he'd have to trek down the road and hope someone else had come up to their cabin this weekend.

He'd turned and taken three steps when he saw another truck. Probably the one Dahlia had come in.

A bird call lifted into the air, and Kyler turned toward the woods. Gray waved at him, and Kyler checked the cabin before high-tailing it over to the other detective.

"I tried to get her not to go in," Kyler said, his chest burning and not only from the sprinting. He felt so far away from himself, from the cabin that had always been his sanctuary.

"Who is it?" Gray asked, pressing his eyes back to the pair of binoculars he'd been using.

"The coyote. I didn't ask his name this time. But he's been using my cabin since I left."

"Smart," Gray murmured as he made tiny adjustments. "We'd already swept it. Been here. We wouldn't come back."

"But I told him I used it all the time." Of course, Kyler had been fibbing at the time. He had no intention of coming up to the cabin once a month when he'd said that. It had just worked out that way. "He hurt my dog." His voice pinched, and Kyler reminded himself to focus on the human casualty of the situation. "We have to get Dahlia out of there."

"We'll have two SWAT teams here in no time," Gray said. "Dahlia's smart and savvy. She'll be okay." He sounded like he was trying to convince himself as much as Kyler.

"Is she armed?"

"No."

Kyler fisted the scissors as a roar came from the house. "He knows I'm gone." Kyler darted out from the trees without thinking. All he knew was that he needed to get to Dahlia before something really bad happened.

The front door opened when he went past the gate, and she came out first, her head held back at an odd angle. Kyler skidded to a stop. "Let her go."

"I told you to stay." The coyote brought Dahlia right to the edge of the steps.

"I'm not your dog," Kyler growled. "Now let the girl go. She's not important." He met Dahlia's eyes, the spark and resiliency there as strong as ever. She kept her right hand up and back, supposedly on the man's hand where he held her by her hair. The other hand balled into a fist, and she lifted her eyebrows as if to say, *Yes? We're good? Should I?*

Kyler wasn't really sure what she was asking, but he nodded.

Dahlia screamed and swung her fist into the man's

stomach at the same time Kyler charged the steps. But she didn't need his help, not really. She yelled as she lifted the doubled-over man over her shoulder with both hands now clenched around the one he'd been using to hold her hair tight.

"There are people in the back rooms," Kyler said, reaching for the open door and pulling it shut. "They work with him."

"Gray!" Dahlia yelled, her chest heaving with her breath, and the man came sprinting forward. "Cuffs. Keep Kyler safe. There are more people inside."

"You can't go in there alone." Gray handed her the cuffs and peered in the window.

"Well, they can't get away." She knelt on the man's back and bent his arms around him to secure him. "Some of them are victims."

"At least two aren't," Kyler said. "Women."

Dahlia straightened. "I'm going in there."

Kyler caught her wrist in his hand. "Dahlia, please don't." Their eyes met, and time slowed for just a breath. "I love you," he said. "And I have a bad feeling about you going in there."

Time rushed forward again, and Gray said, "I'll go." He opened the door before Kyler could protest. He swung his weapon left and right and said, "Clear," before moving farther in.

The man struggled on the porch, and Dahlia put her foot on his back and said, "Stay still. They'll be here for you soon."

He muttered something in Spanish that Kyler was sure was rude. Gray returned a moment later, his phone pressed against his ear. "....scattering to the north and east," he said. "I counted at least eight people. Probably more."

"You'll never find them," the coyote said.

"We found you," Dahlia said. "So don't be too sure."

Gray continued to talk into his phone, his expression one of pure displeasure. Kyler knew they hadn't gotten everything they wanted, but Dahlia was safe. He was safe. He slipped his hand into Dahlia's, glad when she squeezed back.

Only minutes later, two police cars arrived, and McDermott stepped from the car, surprise mixing with seriousness on his face. "Kyler, you all right?"

He realized he was still holding the pair of scissors. He dropped them to the porch, where they clattered against the wood. "Yeah, okay." He released Dahlia's hand and went down the steps. "He did something to BB."

He ran to the little dog lying on the road next to the truck and found his chest rising and falling as if asleep. "BB? Bread and Butter, wake up."

"I'll radio a vet," McDermott said. "Looks like maybe he was drugged to keep him silent." His friend's hand came down on his back. "Don't touch him or move him, Kyler. Okay?"

Kyler wanted to scoop the little dog into his arms and cry, ridiculous as that sounded. "Okay." He nodded and sucked back his emotions, placing just two fingers on BB's chest so the pup would know he was there.

Chapter 18

Dahlia warred with herself. She wanted to stay with the coyote all the way to the holding cell and then the interrogation room. Never let him out of her sight. But Kyler bent over his dog tore at her heartstrings. They sounded a loud note, and she left the coyote with three capable police officers stationed nearby.

She knelt next to Kyler and touched his shoulder. He winced and looked at her with anguish in his eyes.

"Sorry." She leaned her head against his bicep. "For everything."

Kyler sniffed and kept his eyes on the dog. "I'm just glad you're okay."

"Did you mean what you said?" she whispered. The words had been screaming in her ears since he'd said them.

I love you.

"Yes." He put his hand on her knee.

"I'll have to work late tonight," she said. "But maybe after your interview, we can grab some dinner."

He swung his head toward her. "You want to go to dinner?"

"It might be the kind we swing by and get and take back to the office." She blinked at him, the first inklings of a smile pulling against her mouth. "I want to choose you."

If only the fear over the uncertainty of the future would let her.

"It's not me or the job," he said.

"But it is, Kyler." She watched as more police cars arrived, along with a SWAT truck from Vernal. Gray appeared to give them directions, leaving Dahlia to stay with Kyler—right where her heart wanted her to be.

"And I choose you." She pressed her lips to his cheek, never more sure of anything in her life. "I choose you."

TEN MONTHS LATER:

Dahlia watched the clock obsessively until it hit three p.m. Gathering her purse, she said, "I'm off, Lois. I'll see you in a couple of weeks."

The older secretary looked away from her computer. "Two weeks?"

"I'm getting married tomorrow, remember?" Warmth passed through Dahlia. The last ten months had been a whirlwind of emotions and activities. First, she'd stayed on as a Unified Police Force detective just until the case with the coyote had been all stitched tight. Then she'd put in her resignation, without a real plan for what she'd fill her days with.

She'd loved police work her entire life, but somehow now that she had Kyler in her life, she was ready to move on. In a small town like Brush Creek, her options hadn't been too wide or varied, but an office management position had come up at the police department, and Dahlia had been the ideal candidate.

She'd been filing reports, keeping everything organized for the officers, and running training meetings for six months—and she'd never been happier. She went in at eight each morning and she left at five each night. The routine of it all brought peace to her normally chaotic life, and as she stepped into the spring sunshine, she couldn't believe how different her life was now from what it had been a year ago.

And not just because of the diamond she wore on her left hand. She glanced at it, still not quite used to its presence in her life, as well as everything it represented.

She opened the passenger door to Wren's car and said, "Hey. No Etta?"

"My mom took her." Wren grinned at her and pulled onto the street. "Are you ready for this?"

Dahlia giggled with Kyler's sister. "The rehearsal dinner will go fine. I'm more worried my dress won't be ready."

"Oh, they called," she said. "The girl said she can finish the last stitches after she makes sure it fits in the bust." Wren increased her speed once she hit the highway outside of town. "She said it would only be a few minutes."

Dahlia still worried the whole way to Vernal, to the dress shop where she and her mother had chosen the dress she'd be married in tomorrow at eleven. The shop had been working on the alterations for four months, and Dahlia had no idea it took that long to sew in an extra panel in the scoop back or add a few beads.

Wren's phone bleeped, and she handed it to Dahlia. "Just see if it's Tate or my mom."

It wasn't her husband or her mother. "It's Fabi." Dahlia kept reading. "She says she and Jazzy just left." She looked at Wren. "Are they meeting us there?"

"Yeah. I invited them. Is that okay?"

One thing Dahlia hadn't quite been prepared for was the inheritance of four sisters. As an only child, dealing with Kyler's large family had been a challenge, to say the least. But Fabi, Jazzy, and Wren had wanted to be involved every step of the way.

"Yeah, sure." Dahlia had been grateful for their help in picking out flowers, setting the menu for the luncheon, choosing colors, and tasting cakes. Planning a wedding had been overwhelming, but having the Fuller sisters at her side had made it all easier.

Berlin, the youngest Fuller, had been noticeably absent

during most of it, but she was taking online college classes and working full time. Wren had told Dahlia that Berlin had a lot going on and she'd come around eventually.

Dahlia thought there was more going on, but she wasn't marrying Kyler so she could play detective with his family.

She was marrying him because she loved him.

She smiled thinking about him and their big day tomorrow, and the dress fitting went fine. They arrived back in Brush Creek, the pavilion Kyler had spent the last twenty years mowing around decorated beautifully, with the bright yellow and navy blue balloons, as well as white lilies on every table.

The metal picnic tables had been covered with white tablecloths, with navy confetti sprinkled around the vases.

Dahlia paused on the threshold of the pavilion, glad she'd worn the fit-and-flare navy dress with stars and galaxies on it. "This is perfect."

Wren linked her arm through Dahlia's. "I told you the Davis's were the best at parties." She'd recommended Amber Davis as the decorator, and she also supplied all the flowers. Kyler had wanted the wedding outdoors, somewhere meaningful to him, and there was nowhere better than Oxbow Park. Dahlia had spent countless hours on the running paths here, so she had no objections.

"Hey, gorgeous." Kyler swept his arm around

Dahlia's waist and brought her flush against him before placing a kiss on her temple. "How'd the fitting go?"

"Great." She leaned into him. "I have the dress, so I think the wedding will go on as scheduled."

He chuckled and tugged at the navy paisley tie she'd bought for him weeks ago. "Food's here," he said. "They arrived just after me."

Dahlia turned to see several people making their way toward them, pushing silver carts with equipment and long, covered trays of food.

"I can't believe you let me have sandwiches at our wedding." Kyler watched them approach with appreciation in his eyes.

"That's how much I love you." Dahlia wrapped her arms around her almost-husband and giggled. "Plus, I liked Teddy's too." They both liked the restaurant so much, they went every weekend and hiring them to do the wedding luncheon was a no brainer.

"Mom's ten minutes out," Wren said, pushing her phone into her back pocket.

"Oh, my, goodness, look!" Fabi's voice went nuclear and Dahlia followed her frantic gaze to the parking lot.

Dahlia sucked in a breath, as surprised as everyone else staring at the two people walking toward them, hand-in-hand.

"Is that Gray?" Kyler asked.

"And Berlin." Jazzy sounded absolutely gleeful.

"Isn't he like, twice her age?" Kyler looked at Dahlia, his older brother concern evident.

"He just turned forty," Dahlia said, the last word sticking in her throat. She'd known Berlin wasn't telling the whole story. But Gray should've said something to her. Her surprise faded into a slight sting of betrayal that her former partner hadn't mentioned he was getting cozy with the youngest Fuller.

He dropped Berlin's hand as they approached, but he didn't flip back his reflective shades. Berlin smiled at her giddy twin sisters. "I think most of you know Gray Salisbury."

"I certainly do," Dahlia said, stepping into Gray and giving him a quick hug, along with the words, "What in the world are you thinking?"

Berlin had to be no older than twenty-five, and Gray had a fourteen-year-old daughter.

"I'm thinking I'd follow my heart," he hissed back before stepping away and meeting the rest of the Fullers that had already arrived.

"Can I talk to you for a sec?" Kyler wove his fingers through Dahlia's and led her away from the pavilion.

"What's up?" she asked.

"Just wanted to enjoy this moment with you." He lifted her hand to his lips. "Tomorrow at this time, we'll be in Salt Lake City, and then off to Grand Cayman."

A smile burst onto Dahlia's face. "I can't wait."

Kyler paused and leaned down, almost brushing his lips against hers. "Me either. I love you." He kissed her, sending sparks to all of Dahlia's extremities. "Thanks for choosing me."

"I would choose you over and over again," she said.

Kyler grinned. "I'm so glad I waited for that date."

Dahlia was too, and she kissed her almost-husband with love and gratitude in her heart, the best guide she'd ever followed.

————

Read on for a sneak peek at the next novel in the Brush Creek Cowboys series, **THE PARAMEDIC'S PARTNER** - which is 2 love stories in 1 book! You'll get to see both of the twins find their happily-ever-after.

Sneak Peek! THE PARAMEDIC'S PARTNER Chapter One

Fabiana Fuller groaned, the light coming through the window like daggers to her aching head. It was more of a stabbing pain pounding through her temples, and her stomach cramped uncomfortably too.

"Jazzy," she moaned, hoping her twin was still in the room somewhere. She vaguely remembered hearing the squeak of the door as it opened, but that could've been yesterday. Or last year. Maybe another lifetime.

Everything hurt, but Fabi managed to push her legs over the side of the bed and use her hands to get herself into a sitting position. Her vision swam, and she lay back down.

This couldn't be happening, but a late spring flu had been making its way around Brush Creek, taking down the Chief of Police, her mom, the pastor, and now, apparently Fabi herself.

"Jazzy," she tried again, this time rewarded with that squeak that annoyed her sister but that Fabi actually found comforting. After all, no one could come in their shared bedroom silently, and Fabi's overactive imagination sometimes had someone trying to abduct her in the middle of the night.

"You're burning up," Jazzy said, her usually playful voice nowhere near jovial now. "I'll call Wren."

"Wait." Fabi curled her fingers around her sister's wrist. "I have a date tonight."

A beat of silence passed before Jazzy said, "So? You can reschedule."

Fabi shook her head, but that made the whole room spin violently, and she clamped her eyes shut. "I can't. I've already done that twice. He'll think I'm not interested."

"Surely whoever the flavor of the week is will understand the flu." Jazzy spoke with enough bite to add to Fabi's headache. Fabi didn't blame her, but it certainly wasn't her fault men asked her out instead of Jazzy.

"It's that cute paramedic from the park," she whispered to her pillow. "I really wanted to go out with him." And her stupid work schedule over the past two weeks since the pet adoption in the park had kept her from making her previous attempts to meet Max.

She'd been cleaning up flu germs for everyone from the river to the horse ranch up the canyon. No wonder she felt seconds away from passing out.

Somewhere in the haze of her flu-ridden mind, an

idea formed. "You have to go," she said, tightening her grip on Jazzy's forearm.

"No." Jazzy tried to shake her hand away. "He doesn't want to go out with me. Remember how he met us both and only had eyes for you?" So there was some bitterness in Jazzy's voice. Fabi heard it, didn't know what to do about it. Jazzy was the flirt, and she usually got the men to come over and meet the sisters. But it was almost always Fabi who walked away with a date.

Honestly, the whole charade was getting old. Fabi couldn't even count how many first dates she'd been on in the past year. Probably fifty. Maybe more. It was getting to the second date that was hard.

She *could* count those. Two. Two second dates in the past year. Zero third dates. She wasn't sure what was so wrong with her, but somehow, she believed she was fundamentally flawed.

But Max had been different.

"Please," she begged, only able to say one word through the fire in her throat.

"I don't even look like you." Jazzy stopped trying to get away, and Fabi relaxed a little too.

"Go see Starlee. She can replicate my A-line."

"I don't want to dye my hair."

"It's a few streaks," Fabi said, opening her eyes. "Please, Jazzy. If I don't show up or if I cancel again, I'm sure it'll be over."

"Maybe it should be. I mean, if the guy can't understand the flu." Jazzy sat on the edge of the bed and stroked Fabi's hair off her feverish forehead.

"Just one dinner," Fabi pressed, sensing that she almost had Jazzy convinced. Growing up, the twins had loved switching places, going to each other's classes, trying to fool their friends into believing they were someone they weren't.

They hadn't really taken the practice into adulthood, but then again, the situation had never demanded it.

But this one did.

Fabi pictured Max, who was big, broad, and bald. She'd been immediately attracted to him as he worked with the dogs that were up for adoption. She and Jazzy had a cat, and Marbles would definitely not appreciate a canine companion, but Fabi had played her cards just right, showing just enough interest in the dog to capture the attention of the man.

"He's taking me to Clive's," Fabi said, hoping that would seal the deal. Of course, her sister would have to do their normal housework alone—which she hated— and get her hair cut and colored before six-thirty. But it was do-able.

"What about the mole?"

"He won't notice."

"What if he does?"

In moments like this, Fabi wished she could get the fingertip-sized mole behind her right ear removed. "He won't," she said. "Because you'll be witty, and charming, and flirty—you know, you'll be yourself—and he won't notice."

Jazzy fell silent for what felt like a long time. "But that's not how you act," she finally said.

"You're right," Fabi said. "You better pull the flirting back a bit. And the giggling." Her twin giggled entirely too much. "And no kissing him."

"Why not?" Jazzy said, standing. The movement jostled Fabi, who groaned as discomfort swept through her. "You kiss on the first date."

"Not this year," Fabi said.

"Please." Jazzy scoffed and her footsteps moved away from Fabi's bed. "You kissed Mason Limebert last weekend."

"And he didn't call me back," Fabi said, another pinch moving through her that had nothing to do with the flu. So she wasn't perfect. Maybe she came on too strong. Maybe she had a reputation of kissing on the first date and that was all the men in this town wanted.

"Jazzy?" she asked when she didn't hear the squeak of the door.

"I don't think I can," she said.

"Of course you can." Fabi lifted her head and squinted, wondering how sunlight could hurt so badly. "It's totally do-able, Jazzy. Please." She couldn't quite see Jazzy, but she heard the squeak as the door opened.

"I have to go call Wren." The door clicked closed and Fabi let her head fall back to the pillow before pulling the blanket over her eyes to drown out that merciless sun.

Wren managed all the jobs for A Jack of All Trades, the family company that Fabi and Jazzy worked for. They cleaned all the residential accounts in town, in Beaverton, and even up in Maple Mountain. It was Thursday, which mean their schedule was jam-packed, and Jazzy would never be able to get all their work done, get her hair colored, and be ready to meet a man by six-thirty.

Please, she prayed, her fall-back whenever she couldn't quite make a situation do-able in her mind. But God could make anything do-able. *Please have everyone cancel for today.*

If God was a God of miracles, and Fabi believed He was, then when Jazzy called Wren, she'd find out she had plenty of time to get her work finished and get her hair cut into the stylish A-line bob Fabi had adopted three weeks ago, streaks and all.

———

Fabi had a unique talent to think anything was do-able. Jazmin Fuller, on the other hand, did not. The thought of squeezing in a two-hour appointment at the salon had her teeth clenching while she waited for Wren to pick up.

Her sister answered with a harried "Hey, Jazzy," while a toddler screamed in the background. "What's up?"

"Fabi's not getting out of bed today," she said. "She's got the flu." Jazzy wandered back over to the bedroom doorway and peered inside. Fabi lay perfectly still, her eyes closed and her face gray. A prick of concern touched her heart. "I'm not sure she should be left alone, honestly."

Wren exhaled and grunted. Etta quieted, though her soft sniffling could still be heard through the line. "Well, we got lucky," Wren said, her voice slightly muffled. "Dottie and the Fierios canceled for today."

"They did?" Jazzy couldn't believe Dottie Tanner had canceled. Jazzy and Fabi had been cleaning the older woman's house for a decade, ever since she was their youth leader and her husband had passed away. The Fierios were hit and miss, and in the summer, they were sometimes gone for weeks at a time and did cancel their maid service.

"Dottie has gone to her daughter's for the weekend," Wren said. "The Fierios left a message this morning." She tapped on her keyboard. "So that clears up a few hours. You've still got Guy Haskell's place, but you could do it alone. Doesn't he just want his kitchen and bathrooms done?"

"Yeah, and I could go this morning." Jazzy turned away from the bedroom and moved down the short hall and into the kitchen. Marbles sat on the counter, his gray eyes clearly saying, "Breakfast is late."

Jazzy bent to retrieve his bowls and washed them out. "Don't we have the Robertsons too? There's no way I can do their whole house myself." Well, she could, but the completely irrational side of her was actually considering Fabi's insane plea.

"I'll call them," Wren said. "See if we can reschedule for another time."

"The weekend," Jazzy said as she filled the water bowl and put it on the floor. She reached for the cat kibble. "I hate working weekends."

"I can come do it with you," Wren said. "It'll go quick."

Jazzy couldn't argue with that. Wren was an excellent maid, and Jazzy didn't get to spend much time with her now that she was married and had a little girl. She scooped cat food into the bowl and put it beside the water. Marbles jumped down from the counter, his striped tail held high, and padded over to his breakfast.

"So all I have on my schedule today is Guy's place." Plenty of time to get her hair done and even take Fabi's credit card and get herself something cute for a date that night.

I can't believe you're even considering this, she thought to herself. But she hadn't been out with a man in ninety-nine days, something she hadn't said to anyone, not even Fabi. And for some reason, Jazzy really didn't want to hit Day One Hundred.

"Yep, and give me five minutes to check with him and make sure you can come this morning instead of this afternoon. Then you can take care of Fabi the rest of the day."

Jazzy didn't have the heart to tell Wren that really she had time to get a new look in preparation for a date. Instead, she said, "Sure, five minutes," and hung up.

She immediate texted Starlee to find out if she had time to do a cut and color that day. The stylist's response came within seconds and said, *Absolutely. Tell me when.*

Jazzy had to wait to hear back from Wren, and when she did, she sent Starlee another text—*one o'clock?*—still in shock that she was actually considering going out with a man who'd only had eyes for her twin. Well, and his dogs, which Jazzy was sure was actually worse.

———

THE PARAMEDIC'S PARTNER is available now!

The Marine's Marriage: A Fuller Family Novel - Brush Creek Cowboys Romance (Book 1): Tate Benson can't believe he's come to Nowhere, Utah, to fix up a house that hasn't been inhabited in years. But he has. Because he's retired from the Marines and looking to start a life as a police officer in small-town Brush Creek. Wren Fuller has her hands full most days running her family's company. When Tate calls and demands a maid for that morning, she decides to have the calls forwarded to her cell and go help him out. She didn't know he was moving in next door, and she's completely unprepared for his handsomeness, his kind heart, and his wounded soul. **Can Tate and Wren weather a relationship when they're also next-door neighbors?**

The Firefighter's Fiancé: A Fuller Family Novel - Brush Creek Cowboys Romance (Book 2): Cora Wesley comes to Brush Creek, hoping to get some in-the-wild firefighting training as she prepares to put in her application to be a hotshot. When she meets Brennan Fuller, the spark between them is hot and  instant. As they get to know each other, her deadline is constantly looming over them, and Brennan starts to wonder if he can break ranks in the family business. He's okay mowing lawns and hanging out with his brothers, but he dreams of being able to go to college and become a landscape architect, but he's just not sure it can be done. **Will Cora and Brennan be able to endure their trials to find true love?**

The Trooper's Treasure: A Fuller Family Novel - Brush Creek Cowboys Romance (Book 3): Dawn Fuller has made some mistakes in her life, and she's not proud of the way McDermott Boyd found her off the road one day last year. She's spent a hard year wrestling with her choices and trying to fix them, glad for McDermott's acceptance and friendship. He lost his wife years ago, done his best with his daughter, and now he's ready to move on. **Can McDermott help Dawn find a way past her former mistakes and down a path that leads to love, family, and happiness?**

The Detective's Date: A Fuller Family Novel - Brush Creek Cowboys Romance (Book 4): Dahlia Reid is one of the best detectives Brush Creek and the surrounding towns has ever had. She's given up on the idea of marriage—and pleasing her mother—and has dedicated herself fully to her job. Which is great, since

one of the most perplexing cases of her career has come to town. Kyler Fuller thinks he's finally ready to move past the woman who ghosted him years ago. He's cut his hair, and he's ready to start dating. Too bad every woman he's been out with is about as interesting as a lamppost—until Dahlia. He finds her beautiful, her quick wit a breath of fresh air, and her intelligence sexy. **Can Kyler and Dahlia use their faith to find a way through the obstacles threatening to keep them apart?**

The Paramedic's Partner: A Fuller Family Novel - Brush Creek Cowboys Romance (Book 5): Jazzy Fuller has always been overshadowed by her prettier, more popular twin, Fabiana. Fabi meets paramedic Max Robinson at the park and sets a date with him only to come down with the flu. So she convinces Jazzy to cut her hair and take her place on the date. And the spark between Jazzy and Max is hot and instant...if only he knew she wasn't her sister, Fabi.

Max drives the ambulance for the town of Brush Creek with is partner Ed Moon, and neither of them have been all that lucky in love. Until Max suggests to who he thinks is Fabi that they should double with Ed and Jazzy. They do, and Fabi is smitten with the steady, strong Ed Moon. **As each twin falls further and further in love with their respective paramedic, it becomes obvious they'll need to come clean about the switcheroo sooner rather than later...or risk losing their hearts.**

The Chief's Catch: A Fuller Family Novel - Brush Creek Cowboys Romance (Book 6): Berlin Fuller has struck out with the dating scene in Brush Creek more times than she cares to admit. When she makes a deal with her friends that they can choose the next man she goes out with, she didn't dream they'd pick surly

Cole Fairbanks, the new Chief of Police.

His friends call him the Beast and challenge him to complete ten dates that summer or give up his bonus check. When Berlin approaches him, stuttering about the deal with her friends and claiming they don't actually have to go out, he's intrigued. As the summer passes, Cole finds himself burning both ends of the candle to keep up with his job and his new relationship. **When he unleashes the Beast one time too many, Berlin will have to decide if she can tame him or if she should walk away.**

Go up the canyon to Brush Creek Ranch, where a community of retired rodeo cowboys are looking for love...

Brush Creek Cowboy (Book 1): He's a cowboy raising his son alone. She's a widow with a chocolate obsession. **Can Brush Creek cowboy Walker get over his losses and fears in order to build a future with Tess?**

Meet the cowboy billionaire brothers at Seven Sons Ranch. The Walkers are new in Three Rivers, and they've got the women circling. Every contemporary romance in this series features a fake marriage that turns to more, family holiday traditions, and the family saga that will create a space for you in the Walker family too!

RHETT (Book 1): To save her business, she'll have to risk her heart. She needs a husband to be credible as a match-maker. He wants to help a neighbor. **Will their fake marriage take them out of the friend zone?**

Journey to the beautiful Texas Hill Country for heartwarming, clean cowboy romance with that hint of faith you'll love. This series includes an Army cowboy, a cowboy billionaire, seasoned romance between older characters, Christmas romance, and three brothers looking for a ranch and a the woman of their dreams!

Choosing the Cowboy (Book 1): Maggie Duffin is all set to inherit her father's farm supply store in Amarillo, Texas. With only girls in her family, and Heidi now married and living at Three Rivers Ranch, she feels a sense of duty and family loyalty. Which is honorable—if it wasn't for her boyfriend, cowboy Chase Carver.

This is an introductory novelette to the Grape Seed Falls Romance series, with full-length books starting with CRAVING THE COWBOY.

About Liz

Liz Isaacson writes inspirational romance, usually set in Texas, or Wyoming, or anywhere else horses and cowboys exist. She lives in Utah, where she writes full-time, takes her two dogs to the park everyday, and eats a lot of veggies while writing. Find her on her website, along with all of her pen names, at feelgoodfictionbooks.com.